Rose
and the
Rogue

ALSO BY ELIZABETH COLE

Rose
and the
Rogue

ELIZABETH COLE

SkySpark Books

PHILADELPHIA, PENNSYLVANIA

SkySpark Books
Philadelphia, Pennsylvania
skysparkbooks.com
inquiry@skysparkbooks.com

Publisher's Note: This is a work of fiction. Names, characters,
places, and incidents are a product of the author's imagination.
Locales and public names are sometimes used for atmospheric
purposes. Any resemblance to actual people, living or dead, or to
businesses, companies, events, institutions, or locales is completely coincidental.

Ordering Information:
Quantity sales. Special discounts are available on quantity pur-
chases by corporations, associations, and others. For details,
contact the "Special Sales Department" at the address above.

ROSE AND THE ROGUE / Cole, Elizabeth. – 1st ed.
ISBN-13: 978-1-942316-49-7

Author's Note

I must thank my beta readers and my editor, Amanda Valentine, for their suggestions to improve the story. I would also especially like to thank my sensitivity reader, Kerry Kijewski, for her thoughtful comments and notes regarding both practical issues for blind people as well as the social perceptions of the blind, both historical and contemporary. As someone who is not blind, I have done my best to represent Rose as realistically as I can, and any mistakes are fully mine.

ELIZABETH COLE

Prologue

❦

SUNLIGHT FELL ON ROSE'S FACE, warming her cheeks and nose as she tipped her head up toward the source of heat. She instinctively squinted against the powerful beams, which her damaged eyes still registered as too dangerously intense.

"Don't look at the sun," her mother told her.

"I can't look at anything," Rose returned, bitterness marring her otherwise tender young voice. *"I'm blind, Mama."*

"As if we could forget, poor darling."

Without warning, her mother enfolded her in an embrace, and the nine-year-old Rosalind Blake clung to her, wishing that she could see her, but happy she could at least inhale the florals of her mother's perfume and feel the softness of her skin.

Rose very nearly died from the illness that took her sight. On the worst night, the doctors were certain she'd be gone before sunrise…but she lived, and the fever broke, and she slowly recovered. Which was when she learned that she would never see anything again.

"There now," her mother whispered. "Don't cry, my sweet. This school is said to be very accommodating, and came well recommended. You'll enjoy it here."

If they accept me, Rose thought.

Just then, her cousin Poppy slipped her hand into Rose's and gave it a reassuring squeeze. Poppy had taken on the role of being Rose's guide ever since the illness took her sight (Poppy also got sick that winter, but not nearly so badly).

"The place is very pretty," Poppy whispered. "There's a sign by the gate that says Bloomfield Academy for Young Ladies of Quality at Wildwood Hall. It's a big building of red brick, and there's ivy growing all over the walls. It must have been a very grand residence once. There are wings sprawling everywhere. Come, there's a path up to the door. I'll guide you."

Inside the building, a woman ushered them into a parlor and told them Mrs. Bloomfield would be with them shortly. Rose felt more and more wound up, and Poppy had fallen silent, apparently also nervous in the new surroundings.

What if the school rejected her? Where would she go then? Rose couldn't imagine. Her parents were near despair, lacking the temperament to learn how to adapt to a blind child, especially one who had previously been quite independent and required so little supervision. Her father was a barrister who spent much of his time working, and her mother was…well, rather unreliable.

Having Poppy come to live with them helped, because they were fast friends, and Poppy was naturally the sort of person who liked to help others. But Poppy was just a little girl herself, and could not be expected to provide for Rose's education. Hence the search for a proper school for young ladies where Rose might get along.

"Good afternoon," a smooth voice said then, startling Rose back to the present moment. "Welcome to Wildwood Hall. I am Florence Bloomfield, the headmistress."

Rose turned toward the voice, trying to decide what sort of woman would fit the tones. Not very young, but not old either. Maybe her mother's own age? And she sounded full of confidence and poise...which made sense for a headmistress who presided over a whole school of girls.

"Mrs. Bloomfield, is it?" Mr. Blake asked with a shade less confidence than usual. He was on strange ground for him...a world of women. "We are glad to meet you and see the school. This is my daughter, Rosalind Blake, and her cousin Poppy St. George, who would also attend."

Mrs. Bloomfield spoke directly to the girls, her voice still warm and friendly. "Miss Blake, Miss St. George, how do you do."

Rose was already on her feet, having stood at the sound of the new voice, and Poppy was by her side. They chorused back, "How do you do, Mrs. Bloomfield."

"Well, I have no fears for their manners," the headmistress said with a chuckle. "What charming deportment you both have."

And then the talk began, adult talk of attendance and fees and expectations. It flew over Rose's head for the most part.

At one point, her mother was explaining, "She was not born blind. A fever last year took her sight, and it has been...difficult since then."

"Understandable," Mrs. Bloomfield said. "Such a drastic change in one's circumstances always requires a level of fortitude to cope, which Rosalind seems to have done admirably so far. Isn't that correct, miss?"

Rose was surprised to be identified as a person of fortitude, but she replied, "I've done my best, ma'am."

"Wonderful. There will be some challenges, of course,

but much of the curriculum will not need to be changed for you. Perhaps you will not practice painting as some of the girls do, but the letter mentioned that you are fond of music?"

"Yes, ma'am," Rose said. "I like to sing and play the harp and the pianoforte...well, I did."

"No reason why you should not continue here. We have a music room, and an instructor who comes once a week for lessons. I am sure she'd be delighted to have such an eager pupil. Now, let's all take a tour of the building so that you'll know where everything is. I believe it is good for the parents and guardians to know how their girls will be spending their days."

They toured the instruction rooms, the main hall where everyone took meals together, the library, the dormitories. Along the way, Mr. Blake asked again, a little nervously, what sort of things the girls were taught. He clearly worried that Rose's head would be filled with nonsense. (He was a man of his time and had the usual trepidation about women learning too much. That way lay suffrage and all manner of social unrest!)

Mrs. Bloomfield just smiled, having assessed his concerns and prepared a ready answer. "As you already know, the goal of the school is to educate the daughters of the gentry. The girl in the blue dress over there, you see her? Her father is Baron Rutherford."

Mr. Blake made an *mmm*ing sound of recognition, though he was probably just pleased that Rose and Poppy would be rubbing shoulders with girls destined to have titles.

Rose noticed that the woman avoided any mention of what might be taught, and decided she liked the headmistress more every minute.

"Would you like to meet some of the students?" Mrs.

Bloomfield asked Rose, then answered herself. "Of course you would, after listening to grown-ups drone on. Let's get you among your own kind." She raised her voice, calling to a nearby group. "Daisy? Heather? Camellia? Come here, girls! Please introduce yourselves to our newest students."

A moment later, Rose and Poppy were surrounded by a trio of friendly inquisitiveness, and parents and teachers were quite forgotten amid greetings and rapid-fire questioning about favorite colors and books and did they like to play hide and seek and did they know how to plait their own hair in that particularly fancy way, or did a maid do it?

Daisy (the aforementioned baron's daughter) had a soft voice and tended to trail off before actually finishing her sentences. *What pretty ribbons! Are they…silk…?* Heather tended to jump on Daisy's dwindling comments and finish them while hopping to the next question. Heather seemed like a wildfire waiting to happen. *Oh, they look like silk! I say, do you girls like lamb? I think that's what we're having for dinner today. I know where Cook keeps the biscuits she makes for tea in case you ever need a treat, just ask me and we'll sneak in, it's easy!* And then Camellia, or Lia as she instantly announced, would make a sharp observation that suggested she was very used to Heather's antics. *Last time you got your ears boxed when Cook caught you—is a sesame biscuit really worth it?*

Thus, Rose did not hear when her father said to the headmistress, "So you'll take her on, then? It won't be too much inconvenience, if Poppy is here to help her?"

"I am confident both girls will be good students," Mrs. Bloomfield said. "They are already fitting in, as you can tell."

"Oh, I'm so glad," Mrs. Blake sighed. "I wish I knew how to deal with things for her now that she's blind, but I'm just making everything worse! I'm inadequate to the task. When I look at her now and I think of how little I seem to help her, it's all I can do not to cry."

"No call for tears," Mrs. Bloomfield replied. "You have a bright young daughter who is interested in the world and has friends at her side. With those two qualities, one has all one could need."

Chapter 1

The ballroom was crowded, loud, overscented, and overheated...all of which was to say that the party was a success. The din especially was terrific: musicians in one corner, groups of chattering guests along the edge of the dance floor, and the frequent peal of laughter as someone reacted to a particularly amusing joke.

As usual, Rose experienced all of this from the side of the room, with her mother and Poppy nearby. She was not exactly in demand as a dance partner, or even as a conversational partner. In truth, Rose didn't know many people and thus was doomed to remain a wallflower at such events. Poppy was asked to dance three times by various gentlemen, and she accepted each time, but always hurried back to Rose, reporting that the excursion was not worth it.

The most recent dance partner fared the worst in Poppy's estimation.

"I would say he's a peacock," Poppy whispered to Rose so Mrs. Blake wouldn't overhear. "Except that he looks more like a rooster."

Rose stifled her laughter, wishing with all her heart that she could see the person her cousin described. In fact, she wished she could see anything at all. But she was denied many of the simple pleasures her cousin Poppy took for granted...such as being able to survey the ridiculousness of a *ton* ball in London during the height of the Season. Fortunately, Poppy, both cousin and companion, was her invaluable compatriot in the world—and her eyes.

"What is he wearing?" Rose asked eagerly, tapping her walking stick in a rapid beat in her impatience to hear the details. She was young for such an accessory, but Rose didn't use the stick to support her weight. She found it supremely useful to swing a few feet in front of her as she walked, alerting her to obstacles in her path. She'd chosen this particular stick (a slender rod of birch) for its light weight and finial of cool silver metal cast in the form of a rose.

"A bright yellow jacket—mustard yellow," Poppy replied. "And his waistcoat is trussed up so tight I don't think he can breathe, let alone talk. Which may be a blessing for his companions."

Once more, Rosalind covered her mouth with her hand. Her inner vision was filled with the descriptions of the people at the ball that her companion colored in with such detail. She had only the memory of colors, but her imagination was robust, and she was amused at the scene her mind conjured.

"But Mr. Mustard was polite, surely?" she asked.

"Oh, yes, perfectly polite. And perfectly dull! How did you find the food, Miss St. George? Have you ever been to the Lake District, Miss St. George? Do you like to ride, Miss St. George? All of which tells me that *he* likes to eat and go to the Lake District and ride around himself. He didn't really ask anything of me, because he wasn't at all interested in me."

Rose thought that a pity, because Poppy was such a

fun and engaging companion, always interested the world around her and ready with a wise observation on what she found.

"Anyway," Poppy continued, "I didn't like his jacket. The wool was cut-rate." (Poppy's stepfather was in the cloth trade, and she had very strong opinions on fabric.)

"Are all the men like that tonight?" Rosalind wondered. "Trussed up in bright colors, I mean?"

"No, though many are. I wonder if they know how foolish they appear. Doubtless some of the ladies are impressed."

"I take it you are not impressed by any of these fine gentlemen?" she teased her cousin.

"Indeed not!" Poppy said. "I prefer a man who doesn't need to hide behind a fancy jacket. And he must be intelligent. Nor would it hurt if he were built like Adonis."

"Shh," Rosalind warned. "Mother will hear you and have an attack of vapors."

"Aunt Gertrude thinks we're both children still," Poppy said with disdain. "But we're not children, are we? Else why would we be standing at a ball, dressed up like dolls, and hoping to catch a husband before we reach old maid status?"

"You will find a match," Rosalind said, "*if* you don't frighten your potential husband away with your sharp tongue. But I'm selfish, since I secretly hope you do scare them all away. What will I do once you're a wife?"

"Oh, don't go on like that, Rose. You sound like a crabby spinster beyond the reach of men."

"That's exactly what I am," she returned.

"Nonsense." Poppy pressed her hand into Rosalind's emphatically. "I have told you again and again. You're charming and accomplished, and pretty in the bargain. I know there's a man who will understand that you are a treasure, just as I know it and our family knows it."

Rosalind stood still, wishing she believed her cousin. "I'm twenty, flawed, and without suitors."

"So am I. Everyone is flawed."

"But you have received offers of marriage."

"I refused them as fast as I could! I didn't care for Mr. Shankly," Poppy said, speaking of the latest to dare to ask for her hand.

"But at least he cared for you!"

"*Pfft.* He just wanted a clever wife to manage his house."

"Which is more than I could do. How can I be a suitable wife if I cannot be a good housekeeper?" Rosalind had some ladylike accomplishments, mostly having to do with music. But she lacked the ability to handle many household tasks on her own, due to her blindness, and she knew it was a major obstacle for a marriage.

"Marry wealth." Poppy's deadpan tone jolted Rosalind out of her gloom. "Then you'd have all the servants you need to carry out your instructions."

Rosalind sniffed at the idea. "Now that's the most absurd thing you've said all night. Where would I even meet a man so wealthy that he can employ an army of servants?"

"You could meet him anywhere! After all, we have firsthand knowledge that such things happen, or have you forgotten Daisy's wedding already?"

How could she? Their schoolfriend Daisy had been married only a few months ago, in January, and they'd attended the wedding. And, yes, it was true that Daisy married well, for she was now a duchess...but more importantly, blissfully in love.

Rose sighed. "That was a good visit. I'm so happy for Daisy, and I was happy that we all got to be together again, if only for a few days. I fear that we won't have that chance again."

She missed her school days at Wildwood Hall. It had only been a few years since she'd completed her education there, and returned home to prepare for her advance onto the marriage mart. Not that either Rose or Poppy had very spectacular debuts. Rose's parents hosted a party where both the girls were the guests of honor, and it was more or less announced that they were now available to court.

To put it mildly, Rose did not find herself besieged by suitors. She came of good family: her father, Dillon Blake, was a respected barrister in London, and she'd bring a tidy dowry to her marriage. But most men did not want the burden of a blind wife. Thus Rose was very much ignored at these sorts of parties, and she did not expect to ever be courted in the way that other young ladies on the marriage mart were.

Meanwhile, Poppy's thoughts were on more immediate things. "Ooh, there's a very striking man across the room speaking to our hostess. I don't know him, but *he's* got a good tailor, that's certain."

"You've got a funny way of evaluating a man's worth," Rose commented. Indeed, ever since Poppy's mother had remarried, to a tradesman no less, Poppy had begun to participate in her stepfather's business and learn rapidly about all aspects of fabric and sewing.

"Oh, I'm not saying the clothes make the man…just that it's nice when the clothes *fit* the man. And that man is a picture. You should see how everyone is looking at him without seeming to look. I wish I knew his name so we could gossip more about him. His jacket is excellent. Cut just right and a very lovely blue-gray, not dandyish at all. Far better than Mr. Mustard's choices."

Rose smiled, thinking that having Poppy at her side was almost as good as seeing for herself. "We shall surely talk of Mr. Mustard for months to come."

Poppy squeezed her arm. "Ha! I'm about to top it, because someone else just walked in." She proceeded to paint a portrait of a dandy's outfit so hilarious that Rosalind nearly doubled over with giggles.

"Oh, my," Poppy finished, having dissolved into laughter herself. "I should stop. There's a whole group of gentlemen watching us now."

"More dandies?"

"Who else? Oh," Poppy said suddenly. "Bother! One of them is coming toward us!"

"Which one? Not Mr. Mustard again?"

"No, a different man entirely. He's dressed in a black velvet coat. He's handsome," Poppy added, almost as an afterthought.

The heralded man in black velvet did not turn away. Accompanied by the hostess of the party, he had almost reached Poppy and Rosalind before her mother noticed the likely meeting and managed to join the girls.

"Mrs. Blake," their hostess began, "I wish to introduce to you a man I have known for many years."

"Certainly. Any friend of yours…" Rosalind's mother said easily.

"Well, he was quite charmed by the picture of three such lovely women, and begged me to arrange an introduction."

"It's quite true. Good evening, my ladies," the man said. Rosalind heard a sort of laugh in his tenor voice, and wondered if he'd also been mocking the dandies. "Jonathan Hynes, at your service." He bowed first to Rosalind's mother, but instantly turned his attention to Rosalind herself as the girls were named.

"I could not help noticing your angelic appearance, Miss Blake, and your affliction."

He's certainly flowery, she thought.

He went on, "Would it be presumptuous to ask if you dance?"

"I do dance, Mr. Hynes," Rosalind returned before her mother could interject. Not that she was likely to forbid her daughter the chance to find a suitor.

"Then if you would do me the honor?" Rosalind felt him take her arm, rather suddenly. But she was weary of standing along the side of the room with all the forgotten and ignored flowers, so she welcomed the opportunity to join the other revelers.

"Take care of my stick, won't you, Poppy?" she told her friend as she offered the walking stick to her. It would do no good for her during the dance.

Hynes took Rose to the floor, moving fairly carefully through the crowd, though he missed a few warnings that might have saved her toes from running into people. But once on the floor, Rosalind found her natural footing. Rather surprisingly to most people, she was a good dancer (learned from hours of partnering Poppy in the family parlor). She had a gift for memorization, useful for learning the layout of a house, the words of an aria, and the steps of a dance.

Hynes noticed her skill, and about midway through the dance he complimented her, his voice still holding a hint of laughter. "You are very graceful. A surprise from a blind girl."

"Thank you, sir," Rosalind returned, feeling a sudden shiver of apprehension, though she did not know why his words troubled her so much.

"I'll wager that you wouldn't need a partner at all, not the way you move." Again, she caught something unpleasant in his voice.

"I don't know what you mean," she said. "Dancing is not a thing one can do by oneself."

"Isn't it? Let's find out." With those words, he released his hold on her and stepped away with a mocking laugh, leaving her alone.

Despite the stifling warmth of the ballroom, Rosalind felt the departure of Mr. Hynes like a sudden rush of cold air. Without a partner, she was lost in the din of the dancing, the shoes of dozens of partners clicking on the parquet floor, the music swirling around her ears.

A man bumped into her, nearly knocking her down. "Excuse me," he muttered, managing to accuse her of clumsiness with his intonation, even while mouthing the polite phrase.

Recovering her footing, Rosalind wondered which way she ought to walk. She had no idea where her mother and Poppy were, or even which direction she was facing. Where was the musicians' platform? Where were the great double doors?

Another couple brushed past, the woman muttering that *some* people ought to stay home if they couldn't behave at a party.

Rose heard someone else charge by, and stepped to the side before she got trampled.

No one offered to help.

Time stretched on…possibly seconds, possibly minutes.

She stood stock-still, too confused to make a decision. She didn't even know the fastest, safest way off the dance floor. The rush of air round her warned her that other couples were narrowly avoiding a collision. She began to feel the pricking sensation that she was being watched. A blind girl standing alone in the middle of a dance floor! Who wouldn't be watching and laughing?

Then, without warning, she felt herself being swept up into the dance again, her hands caught in the firm grasp of a total stranger.

Chapter 2

ROSE WAS OVERWHELMED BY THE sudden presence of a new body, protectively close to hers as he maneuvered her back into the steps of the dance. Though he said nothing for the moment, the chaos of the dance floor seemed to settle, and Rose was once again part of the pattern.

During a spin that brought the dance partners into each other's arms for a brief moment, she allowed her free hand to float up and rest on the stranger's shoulder, mostly to discover anything about him. He was taller than Hynes, and the lines of his body were more obvious. More muscular.

Still feeling extremely out of sorts, she could only state the obvious. "You're not Mr. Hynes."

"Definitely not. I'm very glad you noticed," the man said, his baritone equal parts humor and anger, even as he moved her expertly around the floor.

"Are you one of his friends?" she asked sharply. "Is this some kind of game?"

"It may have been a game to Hynes, but it is not to me." He squeezed her right hand lightly, as if to reassure her. "My name is Adrian Marsh. I regret that I don't know yours."

"Rosalind Blake," she replied shortly, still not sure she could trust this man, though his name was vaguely familiar. "If it's not too much trouble, would you *mind* telling me what is going on?"

"Can't you see what's going on?"

"No, you idiot, I cannot!"

He stiffened for a moment, then all of a sudden he said, "My God, you're blind, aren't you?"

"Alas, yes," she retorted, embarrassment and anger making her harsh.

"I didn't realize. I just thought…" He sounded so surprised that Rose knew he genuinely didn't recognize the fact until just now.

Then he recovered himself. "Well, let me tell you what I can see, Miss Blake." Marsh continued to move, keeping them in time with the music. "It appears that Hynes and his cronies are across the room, viewing us with considerable disappointment. Certainly they expected a different outcome. I wouldn't put it beyond that group to have placed bets on how many times you tripped on the floor, or something equally distasteful." His tone was one of pure contempt.

"He didn't seem that bad," Rosalind noted. "Until he left me, that is."

"I wouldn't trust Hynes to treat a dog well, let alone a lady." Marsh tightened his grip on her slightly. "I hope you don't mind I kept you dancing. It seemed preferable to simply leading you off in the middle of a set. Less noticeable, that is."

"Are people looking at me?" she asked apprehensively.

"Only as much as anyone will look at a beautiful woman." The words rolled easily off his tongue, and the way he spoke them so close to her ear made her flush, even as she tried to dismiss the obvious flattery.

He went on, "I suspect that most of the guests didn't even notice what occurred, or they've chosen a more benign explanation for Hynes's sudden departure. People spend most of their lives absorbed in their own little worlds."

The music ended before she could reply to that. They both applauded with the rest of the dancers, but Marsh's touch soon returned.

"Would you like to step outside, Miss Blake? It's cooler there...with less scrutiny."

She turned toward him, gauging his tone, weighing the possibility that this would end badly. Then she felt the sticky heat of the room again, and simply said, "Yes, please."

Without waiting a moment longer, Mr. Marsh led her to the garden doors, where a breeze came in to cool the guests. He stepped outside and offered his arm by slipping it toward her own. She took it not with one hand, but both. The gesture would normally have implied a greater intimacy, but for Rosalind, it was simply the safest way to walk in an unfamiliar place.

"Are there stairs?" she asked quietly. "I left my walking stick with my cousin, and it's hard to judge my steps without it."

"Yes, there are six wide stairs down to the path, in about five paces."

She nodded, and he guided her down the steps to a gravel pathway, keeping her to the center as they walked.

"There, you're on the terrace now. No more steps to navigate. So you are here with your family?" he added curiously.

"Yes. Oh, I should have told Mother and Poppy where I am! They'll worry if they can't find me."

"We'll go in shortly," he promised. "I just thought you'd like a moment to compose yourself."

"Thank you," Rosalind said. "And please forgive me. I was very rude earlier, on the dance floor. It was chivalrous of you to rescue me, and I called you an idiot."

"Chivalrous? Me?" He laughed at the suggestion, and his laugh was a sort of pleasant rumble, settling around Rose and making her feel much better about this impulsive decision to trust him.

They walked farther from the house, along a gravel path that crunched under her feet. The night air was a balm, and Rose breathed easier. Without her walking stick, she had to keep quite close to her escort, but she was aware that he was walking slowly and with care to allow her to keep up.

"It was lucky you noticed what happened."

"To be honest, I was watching you," he said bluntly.

"Why?" she asked, mystified.

"We're coming to a bench, Miss Blake. Under a carefully pruned cherry tree, nicely secluded without being completely out of sight of the general crowd, in case you're worried about your reputation. Why don't you sit for a moment? You seem a bit shaky, if you don't mind my saying."

She was still trembling in the aftershock of what had happened, and sitting seemed like a fine idea. He led Rosalind to the stone bench and encouraged her to sit. She relinquished her hold on his arm, now that she had no reason to be escorted. But he sat down beside her in such a way that had he moved one inch closer, their thighs would touch.

"Why were you watching?" she repeated.

"Well, first," he answered, "a beautiful woman will catch anyone's eye. And after I saw Hynes take you to the floor—well, let's say that gave me an extra reason to watch. I know something about his sense of humor," he finished bleakly.

"And you stepped in when you saw him leave me."

"Precisely. His behavior was inexcusable, no matter if you could have seen your way off the dance floor or not. Would you like me to call him out?" her companion asked, almost casually.

"You mean, insist on a duel?" Rose laughed in spite of herself. "I thought only men who are personally insulted are supposed to issue challenges."

"I am personally insulted, knowing that he nearly got away with treating you in such a manner. Besides, the defense of a lady is always grounds for a dawn appointment. Are you quite sure you wouldn't like me to challenge him?"

She caught the teasing, hopeful tone in his voice and smiled. "It's a satisfying thought, I admit, but I would feel awful if you were harmed."

"If anyone would be harmed, it would be Hynes."

"You're very confident. Are you a good shot?"

"Excellent."

"But what if he chose swords?"

"He wouldn't. I'm the best swordsman I know," he said in what was surely a jest. Who practiced fencing anymore, as if this were still the era of derring-do and old-fashioned chivalry? "Duels are conveniently scheduled early, so it'd be over by breakfast, and I could take you for a ride in the park afterward."

Rose shook her head at the thought of this mysterious man defending her honor and then whisking her away. "The incident is not worth such bother. Indeed, it would elevate Mr. Hynes beyond what he deserves, which is to be forgotten."

"As you wish, Miss Blake," he conceded. "I shall skip the duel, and just call to take you to the park tomorrow."

She tipped her head, her ear toward him so she wouldn't miss the nuances in his speech. She said, "You know, I almost believe you."

"Believe me entirely."

"I might, if I knew you."

"Ah, there's the rub. Here I am, a stranger in the night, and you are very rightly hesitant. Luckily, it is proper for a gentleman to call upon a lady after dancing the night before. My mother did raise me well, though if you asked her, she'd claim the result was a failure. Where do you live, so that I may fulfill my obligation?"

She told him, not really thinking that it would matter. This man seemed to be one who did not care for rules, a thought she voiced out loud.

"Rules are generally boring," he agreed. "But I obey them when it suits me."

"A very manly position," she murmured. "If I broke a rule, the result could be disaster."

"Yet you allowed me to take you out here," he noted.

"Well, as you said, I did need to recover myself. Mama is going to have a fit either way, so I may as well take a moment to cool down before the next battle."

"It was disgustingly hot in there," he agreed. "I hate parties."

"Then why attend them?" she asked, curious at the contradiction.

"Favor to the hostess. She's done me a few good turns, and my appearance at her soirees is a small price to pay for that kindness."

"She is very kind," Rose said. "She keeps inviting my family in hopes I'll find a suitor at some point." Rose then realized he might think she was angling. "Oh, not that I'm attempting to entrap you!"

He only chuckled. "It would be a very roundabout attempt, Miss Blake, considering I asked you to join me out here, rather than the other way around. You have no suitors?"

"Not a one. I shall die a spinster. And I don't even spin," she added, unconsciously echoing an old running joke she had with Poppy.

"That seems an incredible loss," he murmured.

At that moment, Rose felt him run a finger along her jawline, very gently. She went still, partly from surprise, but also because it was a tantalizing sensation, sending rivers of warmth along her veins.

"I don't even know you," she whispered, a feeble protest when her whole being suddenly ached to be closer to him. She knew she should stop his presumptuous behavior immediately, but found herself unable to muster any retort. His scent, both spicy and warm, rolled over her when she inhaled. It was so different from anything else she could remember, masculine and mysterious.

"I'm easy to get to know," he murmured back.

Rose knew what would happen next, but was still unprepared when he caught her face in his hands, then bent to brush her lips with his own.

Rose had been kissed before, rather often in fact. Men liked to take advantage of her blindness, and frequently tried to see how far they could press her. She always corrected such misapprehensions with cold finality.

But this kiss was different. Her body reacted instantaneously to his mouth on hers, her pulse quickening. As if he knew how sensitive she was to touch, he kept the kiss light—but not innocent. His mouth almost hovered over her own, sometimes pulling back so only his breath touched her lips. It was intoxicating, and she felt her body beg her to succumb to it, to let this encounter go where it would.

Then, he began to rein in the kiss, slowly letting her come back to herself, letting their bodies disentangle. Though they were both still sitting with perfect propriety—–well, nearly perfect—on the bench, she'd felt just how much they had reacted to each other, how easily they had meshed.

"Why did you do that?" she whispered.

"You looked as if you needed a kiss," he said, sounding far too calm when her own nerves were jangling like an out-of-key orchestra. "I'd apologize for doing so, but then we'd have to admit that it happened, and we should probably avoid that."

"Indeed," Rose breathed, thinking that her mother would faint if she heard about her daughter getting kissed in a garden by a stranger.

He found her hand in the darkness. "Let me take you back to your family. I wouldn't want them to worry." He rose and offered his arm, now the solicitous protector again.

Rosalind stood, gripping his arm rather more tightly than before. Absently, she ran her free hand over her hair and dress, hoping to smooth what must be a rumpled appearance.

"You look just fine," he said quietly as he led them back to the house. "More than fine, in fact. No one would ever suspect you'd just…well, never mind. As we agreed, nothing happened."

"Nothing at all."

"You remain happily on your road to spinsterhood, which still seems an incredible loss," he went on. "Men don't get such a silly label. Though *bachelor* doesn't make much sense either. A batch of what, I ask you? Oh, those steps are coming up again, Miss Blake. Six of them, first one just...now...there you go."

"Thank you," she said, then added, "I hope you are a bachelor. That is, I hope you don't kiss girls in gardens when you've already got a wife."

"Miss Blake, I'm wounded! Of course I haven't got a wife. It's rather a point of contention with my mother, as the whole world...knows...except for you..." He trailed off, then said, "You don't know who I am, do you?"

"You introduced yourself as Adrian Marsh, and I did assume you were telling the truth," she said, exasperated all over again.

"I was, but there's a bit more to it—"

Before he could say more, a very familiar voice interrupted. "Rosalind, where have you *been*?"

Her mother had found them.

Chapter 3

MOTHERS WERE ADRIAN'S NEMESIS.

And Miss Blake's mother was *not* been pleased to see her with him.

To say that Adrian was not the person Rosalind's family was expecting to meet would be an understatement. Mrs. Blake's jaw dropped open when she saw him, and the young lady standing nearby held a walking stick, despite not looking as if she required it, and Adrian realized she must be the cousin Rose spoke of.

"Mrs. Blake, I presume," he said politely upon facing the older woman, who was handsomely gowned in a light yellow dress that suited her dark hair, barely touched with gray. He could see echoes of Rosalind's features in this woman's face. "I do not believe we have met. I am Adrian Marsh, Viscount Norbury, at your service."

"Where is Mr. Hynes?" Mrs. Blake blurted, too flustered to cover her confusion.

"Ah, yes. Hynes." Adrian smiled benignly. He squeezed Rosalind's hand, still resting on his arm, imperceptibly. "I cut in on the dance floor, I'm afraid. Utterly improper of me, of course. I beg your forgiveness."

"There is nothing to forgive...my lord," Rosalind said,

squeezing his arm rather hard as she uttered the *my lord*. It was an unspoken rebuke of his lapse, and while the pinch did hurt a tad, he liked that the lady chose to deliver her opinion this way, instead of through a tirade.

"In that case," Adrian said, carefully aiming his comment to Mrs. Blake, "I will return your daughter to you, knowing that my lack of manners has not completely hardened her opinion against me." He drew Rosalind's hand to the other young lady's, so that she would continue to have a guide.

"Are you Miss Blake's cousin?" he asked, knowing that the mother was far too flustered to deal with the dilemma of whether or not to introduce him to the lady.

The younger blonde woman lifted her face to acknowledge him, and he saw the barely contained laughter in her eyes.

"I am her cousin *and* companion, in fact," she said, clearly enjoying the situation. Her expression was almost impish. "Poppy St. George."

"A very appropriate name for a protector, Miss St. George." He smiled at her as she extended her hand. He took it, pressed it briefly, and then placed it in Rosalind's. "Let all men with unkind intentions be wary of you."

Miss St. George looked very pleased at his unusual compliment, which distracted her from noticing when Adrian ran a finger along the inside of Rosalind's gloved arm under the pretense of handing her over to Poppy. He didn't want the girl to forget him, after all.

"Are you all right, Rose?" Poppy murmured, almost too low for Adrian to catch. "I've got your stick right here, whenever you want it."

"I'm fine," she replied, leaning into her friend with the easy intimacy of a sister.

"It was very kind of you to escort her back." Mrs.

Blake had found her voice at last, and she was quickly assessing the situation. "Girls, I think it's time we returned home. Good evening, my lord."

He watched with amusement as the mother hen herded her chicks away from his dangerous presence. He didn't have to guess if Mrs. Blake had heard of him. From her expression of pure horror when she heard his name, it was obvious that his past was well known to her. He was actually surprised she hadn't fainted on realizing that a rakehell like him had gotten within ten paces of her daughter.

That was why he'd left off his title when rescuing Rosalind on the dance floor, in fact. It was so obvious that Hynes was toying with her that he didn't want to add fuel to the fire by advertising the fact that he was Lord Norbury, a name known to all the gossips, and one that a young lady like Rosalind Blake should avoid.

But by the end, it was clear that Rose did not have any idea who or what he was. Adrian felt bad for kissing her. Wait, no. He didn't feel bad about *that*. That part was a pleasure. The way she'd responded to him, and how she'd actually started a little hum in her throat that he could feel more than hear...well, he hadn't been so tempted to continue his explorations in years.

However, Rose was clearly not his sort. She was an innocent girl who lived in another world. So he'd done the proper thing and returned her to the protective shield of the crowd, well before anyone could notice or comment on their brief departure from the ballroom.

After seeing Rosalind and her family leave, Adrian turned back toward the crowd, scanning the room for any trace of Hynes. There he was, dressed in black, like a bad omen. Adrian caught a poisonous look from the other man, who was standing with his friends in a corner, no doubt steaming over the fact that Adrian had disrupted their little game.

What an ass, Adrian thought. It was one thing to mock the conventions of polite society and make fun of the staid balls and events—Adrian did that all the time. But to deliberately humiliate a girl just because she couldn't even see the trick that was coming...that was another thing entirely. It was downright cruel, and Adrian despised cruelty in all forms, considering it a sign of a warped and weak person.

Though Hynes was still glaring at him, Adrian dismissed the cad from his mind. With no more damsels to save, he left the party in search of more exciting diversions. He'd only attended as a favor to Lady Herbert, a longtime acquaintance who appreciated it when her parties had a little more flair than most, such as when a notorious rake dropped by.

But such parties were not his preferred pastime. Even now, he mentally sorted through the possibilities. In addition to the gaming hells and underground boxing matches that gentlemen could enjoy on any given night in London, Adrian also had a number of standing invitations to more private amusements. He thought of one, issued by a lady recently returned from the Continent. He'd had a torrid affair with her a few years ago. But he refrained from calling a carriage to take him to the lady's home in town. He wasn't in the mood for that.

He moved to the front hall and gestured for one of the footmen to call for his carriage. In the time while he was waiting for it to arrive, he chatted with a few more guests and bid the hostess good-night.

"You're a dear to spend a few hours here," Lady Herbert told him. "And don't think I missed how you danced with Miss Blake, though I only caught a glimpse. She really is a darling, and you've done wonders for her caché, I'm sure."

"I doubt Mrs. Blake feels that way, especially considering I was not an approved partner."

"Oh, phew. People noticed, and that's what matters. The worst thing that can happen to an unmarried woman is to be ignored."

"The horror."

"You wouldn't understand, Lord Norbury. No one has ever ignored you." She gave him an arch look, then pursed her lips in mock anger. "I suppose you're off to some wild pursuit now. Gambling or racing or some ungentlemanly fun."

"In fact, I'm going home. My mother leaves for Bath tomorrow and I'd hate to miss a moment of her company."

"Scoundrel! Give her my best wishes. The city gets so dull at the end of the Season. All the interesting people leave for the country."

"I'll let her know she'll be missed." Just then, the footman returned, bowing as he announced the lord's carriage was outside. "Good evening, Lady Herbert."

While the carriage rattled along the streets, Adrian kept thinking of Rosalind Blake. What a strange succession of events brought them to that garden bench. They both had to be at the same party. She had to be asked to dance. Her partner had to be an utter cad. Adrian had to notice her from across the room, *and* trust his instinct that something wasn't right…

"Arrived, sir," the footman announced as he pulled the door open and dropped the little hinged step on the carriage.

That put a stop to his musings, and Adrian stepped out, breathing in the cool spring air as he looked up at his house.

The London home of the Lords Norbury (starting from the fifth viscount in 1690) stood in glorious isolation at the end of its street. Tall trees obscured the property from prying eyes. Adrian liked it that way.

His mother had already retired for the night, so Adrian told the lady's maid that he would make a special effort to rise early in the morning before his mother left for Bath.

"She said you'd not even come home before dawn, sir," the maid informed him.

"Well, in that case, don't tell her I'm here, and I'll be a surprise."

Adrian went up to his bedroom suite where his valet drew a bath and set out everything Adrian might need or want for bed. Sunk up to his chest in the piping-hot bath, he slowly sipped an excellent brandy and recalled the evening.

Well, one specific aspect of the evening. For some reason, his mind was still on Rosalind Blake. He'd noticed her only by accident. His attention had been caught by the sight of Hynes leading an unknown lady to the dance floor. From something in the pair's attitudes, and the way the woman walked...Adrian couldn't put a finger on it, but he didn't like it.

That was what kept Adrian's attention, for what was the odious Hynes doing with such a young woman? True, the lady was a picture, with a figure a nymph would be proud of, set off by the simple lines of the latest Continental-inspired fashion. Dark curls tumbled down around a heart-shaped face. Even across the room, Adrian could almost feel the weight of those curls in his hands, their silky texture between his fingers. Maybe Hynes was simply enjoying dancing with a pretty girl. But somehow, Adrian didn't think so.

When the couple began to dance, Adrian saw the lady

shiver, even from this distance. As if sensing a storm, he began to move toward the floor, not taking his eyes from the couple. Though he knew nothing of the woman, he knew about the man she danced with. That was more than enough.

And it turned out to be prescient, for Hynes's intentions proved to be worse than Adrian guessed. Leaving a woman alone in a crowd of spinning, shifting strangers? What a despicable move.

So without a second thought, Adrian stepped in to save the girl. And he was glad he did, for Rosalind Blake was well worth saving, and an interesting companion.

Only after he had her in his arms did he realize the full truth, and the abysmal depth of Hynes's trick. She was blind. Why the hell hadn't anybody else noticed, and stepped in to help the moment she was left alone?

Well, Adrian could be a rescuer for a night. He'd taken her to the garden to give her a moment to compose herself, but it was very tempting to keep her there, to learn more about this new face. In the brief time they were together, he noticed the way she turned her head so that her ear was closest to him, allowing her to better hear his words. It had been some time since a woman expressed much interest in his words.

Though to be honest, he proved to be equally intrigued by her adorable mouth, the lower lip a little fuller, which was his favorite, since it provided such a lovely target to lick and tug at with his teeth, setting up that hum in her throat…

Damn. This woman had gotten under his skin. Good thing he returned her to her mother when he did! Adrian didn't want this young woman's ruin on his conscience.

* * * *

The next morning dawned bright and clear. Adrian woke up feeling a bit restless, called his valet, and flung on his favorite dressing robe, a slightly tattered garment of layered and quilted silk with dozens of mythical beasts embroidered all over the back and chest and sleeves. One of his first lovers gave it to him as a gift, and Adrian thought he might possibly choose to be buried in it.

Thus garbed, Adrian walked down the main stairs to the vast foyer of the house, tapping his fingers along the solid oak balustrade as he did so.

An older woman standing in the foyer turned to him, and in an acerbic tone said, "Is this a mirage before me, or did my wayward son actually wake before noon?"

"Before noon, and in my own house, no less." Upon reaching her, Adrian gave her a kiss on the cheek. "You didn't really think that I wouldn't see you off, Mama?"

"Hmmph," she said, but was clearly pleased. "Despite that ratty robe, you look well."

"My one talent," he responded dryly. Adrian was well aware that he was attractive, because he'd used that trait to get whatever he wanted out of life. He realized suddenly that Rosalind Blake couldn't possibly be susceptible to his physical appearance. Perhaps if he were to encounter her again, he'd fail to impress her. What if she'd reconsidered the whole evening, and decided that Adrian was not a charming rescuer, but just another opportunistic man eager to get her alone in the dark?

"Are you even listening, Adrian?"

"Of course. What did you say?"

The dowager viscountess lifted her hands to the heavens. "Why do I even bother with such a recalcitrant youth?"

"It's early," he protested. "Tell me again."

"I was saying, dear boy, that while I am gone, you

might take some time to think about what we discussed before."

"Before?"

"Marriage!" she told him in exasperation.

Lady Norbury (as she was still addressed) wore a gown of gray silk, accented with jet beads and lace. She'd never entirely given up mourning for her late husband, who passed away nearly a decade ago. She was still far from elderly, though her hair was now silvery-blond and her frame was a little more frail than he remembered as a child. His mother's eyes were the same green as his, and they were as sharp as ever. Seeing them together, it was quite clear they were family. In fact, they were more or less the only family left in the Norbury line. This fact weighed heavily on his mother's mind.

Adrian didn't want to talk about this topic, and certainly not before breakfast. "Mama, this will come as a complete shock to you, I know. But I have no wish to bind myself for life to a woman that I have no interest in, nothing in common with, and who is merely using me for my title."

"Oh, my boy, how can you be so sentimental? This is society. You must accept it. All your predecessors did."

"And look at the joy in their faces." He gestured to the gallery they stood in, generations of stiffly dressed aristocrats with stern expressions, and nary a smile among them.

"There are some very sweet young ladies out there. Just find one!"

"Sweet ladies want nothing to do with me."

"And whose fault is that, eh? I warned you, your father warned you! But no, you never listened and you behaved terribly, and now you realize that actions have consequences. Thank God that is all behind us now. You nearly killed me, Adrian. My nerves are not what they once were…"

"Your nerves must have once been granite."

"They had to be, considering my trials. And though you've improved in some ways, you've grown worse in others. Running about with anarchists and pirates and revolutionaries…"

"Do you mean Carlos?"

"Yes, that miscreant! De la Something or Other."

"De la Guerra. And he's not a pirate." At least, Adrian had never definitively *proven* he was a pirate…and he aimed to keep it that way. "He's my very good friend since our school days."

"Hmmph. You've chosen friends poorly in the past."

"True. But Carlos is entirely different, and anyway, you like him."

She sniffed. "Nonsense. I did not achieve what I have in my life by liking every charmer who wandered by."

The dowager viscountess had by all measures made a success of her life. Even Adrian's scandals couldn't touch her. She poked at his chest with one finger. "Now you listen to me. I'm off to Bath to take the waters, and by the time I return to town in the autumn, I expect to meet your intended."

"Or what? You'll disown me? I'm the only heir you've got."

"I won't disown you. But I'll be *very* disappointed."

Adrian hated disappointing his mother. And she knew it.

And there was the memory of Rose again. Sitting with her in the garden, while she explained how she wasn't trying to trap him into marriage! And her kissably soft mouth…

"Very well, Mama. I'll grab the nearest woman to

catch my fancy."

"You'll do no such thing. You'll propose to a woman who will add luster to the name of Norbury. Nothing less than perfection will do."

"Perfection is a high bar." His mother would probably dismiss the very idea of a blind woman as an option, Adrian thought. Then he shook his head. What was he thinking? He'd barely met Rosalind Blake. He certainly wasn't going to rush off and marry her!

That would be scandalous.

Chapter 4

DEAR DAISY,

You may think you have a monopoly on meeting aristocrats under odd circumstances, but I must inform you (via my amanuensis Poppy) that it is no longer so. Last night, we attended a party at Lady Herbert's, and not only was I asked to dance by a gentleman *guest, I ended the dance on another man's arm! Shocking, yes, but more so when I learned that my new escort was none other than the Viscount Norbury, a man with more scandals attached to his name than any other in London. However, he is a good dancer and he was very kind to me. I wanted to tell you of the incident in case you might hear of it, even so far as you are from London. Truly, it was only a dance and a short turn in the garden, and with any other companion it would not rate a comment. But the viscount, apparently, stirs up comments whenever he comes within twenty paces of a woman. Poppy tells me that Mama almost collapsed on the floor when she saw me on the viscount's arm. And of course she took us all home straightaway, lest I be asked to dance again by anyone! All in all, it was a memorable evening, to say the least. Though I am certain that I will never encounter Lord Norbury again, I can say I danced with a rake, which is not a milestone I ever anticipated passing on my journey through life...*

"You're not going to tell her about Hynes's actual role in this event?" Poppy asked, pausing in her writing. It was early the next morning, and the girls were in their sitting room adjacent to their shared bedroom, wearing the loose, comfortable dressing gowns they preferred for days at home. Rose's gown was done in a soft, breezy linen, with little leaves embroidered at the neckline and the hem. She ran her fingers over the raised threads, counting the little leaves as she went. Poppy, who liked vivid colors, told Rose that she was wearing a deep red gown this morning.

The day was bright, the warm sun streaming in from the open balcony door, which faced east. Rose and Poppy usually woke up early, and they had a habit of chatting or writing letters or of Poppy reading aloud from the newspapers before they went down to breakfast.

"It's not pleasant to remember Hynes's role," Rose said in reply to Poppy's question. "Honestly, I'd rather not name *him* at all."

"Fair enough," Poppy said. "Anyway, as you say, with any other gentleman, it would not rate a comment. So Norbury whisked you off the dance floor for a few minutes! I am sure that within a week, only you and I will remember that it occurred."

"Mama will remember."

Poppy chuckled. "Yes, Aunt Gertrude will take this memory to her grave! Her darling girl on the arm of the most scandalous rogue in London. Her expression when she saw him...!"

"Tell me again what he looked like. I'm trying to picture it."

"He was the one I spotted earlier, in the very well-cut clothing. The blue-gray velvet jacket was so lovely."

"Poppy. Forget the clothes! What does *he* look like?"

"Handsome," Poppy summed up unhelpfully.

"*Poppy!*"

"Oh, fine. He's just over six feet, and not a bit of him fat. Broad shoulders and all that."

Rosalind had sensed that part already. "Yes, I know he's tall. But what color is his hair? Eyes?"

"His hair is dark brown, with a little red in it. And his eyes are very green, like Aunt Gertrude's emeralds. Do you remember them?"

"Oh, yes." As a young girl, Rose had frequently stared into the emeralds of a necklace that her mother owned, mesmerized by the shifting deep greens. It was one of her strongest visual memories.

Poppy went on, "I'm sure most women would agree that he's got a nice smile too. He was practically laughing when we met, and he returned you to us. I think he was enjoying himself immensely."

"Immensely," Rose echoed, smiling at the lingering memory of the kiss she'd received from him. It had been worth it, she decided, even if it meant she had to endure Hynes's attempt to humiliate her previously.

It was even worth enduring her mother's litany of complaints about the dissolution of all good manners among the *ton*. The ride back home last night had been taxing to say the least.

In the carriage, Rose answered her mother's hysterical questions about the Viscount Norbury and his behavior over the few minutes he'd been with her. Rose dutifully related the story of Hynes's disappearance and Norbury's rescue with little embellishment. (Though, not being a fool, she left out the kiss in the garden. That decision turned out to be a wise one, considering her mother almost succumbed to the vapors as it was.)

At home, the girls were sent to their bedroom immediately. Rose kept her hand on the varnished railing, automatically counting the steps (fourteen, and the third from the top always squeaked). But once in their room, they had no intention of sleeping, and Poppy insisted on hearing every detail over again as they changed into night shifts and loosed their hair for brushing.

"What did Mr. Hynes do, exactly? I know you didn't tell Auntie everything."

Rosalind related the prank in full (her cousin *not* being known for fainting), and heard Poppy gasp with indignation.

"What an awful man! And he seemed so polite when he spoke to us all."

"Well, first impressions do not always hold true," Rosalind said. She thought again of Norbury. Her first impression of him was that he was something of a knight for stepping in to help a girl he didn't even know.

But apparently he, too, was not what he seemed to be. She sighed. At least she understood his kiss now—a rake wouldn't think twice about playing with a woman's affections. In fact, he probably hadn't even realized he was doing it. But Rosalind couldn't forget his touch. It was just as well, she thought, that she would never meet him again. He was a walking scandal; she was a proper young woman. But in the darkness, sleep eluded her, and her thoughts were not proper at all.

Luckily, a new day brought new life, and Rose was in a good mood as she and Poppy walked downstairs to the breakfast room after they finished the letter to Daisy.

The elder Blakes were there already. Rose smelled the strong coffee her father favored in the mornings, and heard the rustle of the early newspapers as he flipped through them in search of items of interest.

"There's our girls," Mr. Blake said as they entered. "Looking as lovely as ever!"

"Morning, Papa," Rose returned as she went to her usual seat. "I assume you have heard what happened last night."

"You mean the little event that nearly destroyed your poor mother's nerves? Why yes, I did hear something about that." He chuckled, evidently not too concerned about the ramifications. Mr. Blake was a barrister, and it took a lot to rile him up. Arguing before the bar tended to sharpen one's ability to take bad news in stride, considering there was always someone on the other side working to undermine your own efforts.

"It's not something to take lightly, Dillon," her mother said from her own chair. "That man is nothing more than a stack of scandals with a title."

"What sort of scandals, exactly?" Poppy asked, eagerness in her voice.

"I told you both last night in the carriage," Mrs. Blake replied. "He's a rake. A rogue. A…"

"Rapscallion?" Poppy supplied, putting a plate with toast in front of Rose.

"Rascal," Mr. Blake added.

"Reprobate," Rose said.

"Oh, good one, darling," her father noted.

Mrs. Blake huffed out in frustration. "None of you are taking this seriously."

"Perhaps *you*, light of my world who I am privileged to call wife, are taking it too seriously," Mr. Blake said in a gentle tone. "It sounds as if this Norbury character livened up the party with an unusual appearance on the dance floor, with our Rose no less. But as that is hardly the level of scandal he's better known for, it will be forgotten soon enough."

"What sort of scandals is he usually known for?" Rose pressed.

"Not the sort that are suitable for your hearing, girls," Mr. Blake said more soberly. "Over the years, Lord Norbury has dallied with more women than we have years together, and has had affairs that have truly shocked the *ton*, which takes some doing. Your mother never would have let you dance with him if he'd asked first. What am I saying? He'd never even be introduced to you!"

Rosalind protested, "He was a perfect gentleman." Well, that wasn't *quite* true. There was his stolen kiss, and the way he subtly caressed her when they said goodbye.

"I am gratified to hear it," her father said. "But the fact remains that his behavior is the talk of the *ton*, and he seems to relish thumbing his nose at society. This is not an acquaintance I would condone for either of you girls."

"I can't imagine why Lady Herbert invited him," Mrs. Blake said.

"He said she likes the notoriety when he appears," Rose told them. "And obviously it works, for her party is over, and here we are still talking about it."

Mrs. Blake sniffed in disapproval.

Rose's father pushed his chair away from the table with a scraping sound. "Well, I must get moving. The Marberry case is proving to be even more convoluted than we feared, and I have considerable work to do before I'll feel ready to argue it with any hope of winning."

"You'll triumph, Papa," Rose said. "You always do."

"Would that all judges were so sympathetic." Mr. Blake kissed Rose on the forehead as he passed, then said to his wife, "Tru, I'll likely be late home tonight. Don't hold the meal, or else you ladies might starve."

"Yes, dear," Mrs. Blake said. "I'll tell Cook to have a cold plate ready for you when you do come home."

After he left, Mrs. Blake reminded Rose and Poppy that she had a meeting at church, where she chaired the committee on aiding the poor. In the years since Rose lost her sight, Mrs. Blake had gone from a rather flighty person to someone who took a keen interest in the world around her. It started with her growing obsessed with the obstacles Rose faced. She cataloged everything from muddy, potholed paths to the severe lack of books for girls in Rose's situation—for a long time, the only materials available to the young Rose were some books of the Bible, the words printed above deeply embossed symbols on paper that Rose could run her fingers over and sighted people could read along with. Night writing (as it was known) was a godsend, but Mrs. Blake felt that more was needed. She even wrote to publishers to demand more be printed.

From there, her interests had moved beyond her own daughter (who was well-cared for and in actuality quite able to negotiate the world around her). Now Mrs. Blake worked through the church to fund efforts to help the poor and elderly, the insane and the disabled. Rose was proud of her mother, though she never told her so, for it might bring up the painful past when Mrs. Blake had temporarily given up in the face of Rose's disability, instead sending her away to school.

"What's on the agenda for the charity work today?" she asked her mother.

"We're bundling wood and fuel for the poor in the parish. Thank goodness the spring is finally here, for the cold is the worst thing to fight. We can supply people with food, but no one can stop the winter."

Not that Mrs. Blake hadn't tried. She directed the knitting of blankets and somehow managed to have a huge shipment of firewood—not coal—sent to the church to be distributed to those in need. However, even that massive supply had been depleted by last month, and Mrs. Blake had grumbled at every day with bad weather since.

She left for church, promising that she'd be back in the afternoon. "Do stay out of trouble, girls," she said by way of goodbye.

Rosalind wondered if she would share her horror story of the previous evening with the other matrons. If Lord Norbury was that bad, she might hold her tongue—unless she wanted to risk another attack of nerves. On the other hand, it was the most exciting thing to happen to the Blake family in years.

Since Rose's piano instructor was expected this morning, the girls changed into outfits suitable for such an event. After Rose's lesson, however, the girls could lounge in the parlor at leisure, since social calls to the Blake house were quite rare.

As she and Poppy were in the parlor, each enjoying a bracing cup of tea, the maid came in with a card on the tray. She glanced at Rosalind, but brought the tray over to Poppy. "A caller for Miss Blake."

Poppy nodded as she took the card. She sounded a little confused when she read the name. "Mr. Evans. He spoke to us at the ball last night. Oh, Rose!" Without a parent figure to guide them, the next step was not at all clear. "I suppose we must say we're not at home?" she asked Rosalind tentatively.

"Oh, why wouldn't we let him in?" Rosalind said a bit impatiently, her tone masking the excitement fluttering up inside her. The notion of a gentleman calling was so unusual, and Rose craved the novelty. "We're both here, and the servants are here as well. What could possibly happen?"

"Very well," Poppy said. "Alice, give us a moment to

look presentable. Then show him in."

"Yes, miss." The maid nodded and hurried out.

Mr. Evans was the first to call that day, but not the last. Rose found herself suddenly beset with callers, nearly all gentlemen whom she scarcely knew.

Alice was kept busy bringing tea, and Poppy and Rose suddenly found themselves hosting a veritable salon, summoning up every scrap of news and *on dit* to keep the conversation going with these near strangers. Luckily, talk did not devolve to discussion of the weather.

The men were all polite and deeply interested in Rose, telling her that it was such a pleasure to meet her before, and they hoped to gain the favor of her attention soon. One asked her if she liked opera and would like to attend a performance (she loved it, but demurred to say so, not certain if this was an actual invitation). Another asked how often she went to Vauxhall Gardens (quite often in spring and fall, as her whole family enjoyed it). Oh, her *whole* family, he'd echoed, disappointed.

Mr. Evans, the first caller and the one who stayed longest, had told her that he'd very much like to take her for a ride in the park one day soon, which was honestly the most reasonable suggestion she heard. She told him that sounded very nice, just as Poppy was herding all the visitors out of the parlor, strongly hinting that they were close to exceeding the time limit of polite visits.

"There must be some mix-up," she said, after Poppy had looked at the cards of three *more* gentlemen who were waiting in the foyer, and reported their names to Rose. "They are all complete strangers to me. Do you know any of them?"

"Can't say that I do." Poppy turned to the maid and instructed her to send the men away. "Tell these men and anyone else who calls that Miss Blake is not at home.

Thank goodness visiting hours are almost over!"

"Mama is going to have a fit when she hears you turned suitors away."

"How could they be suitors? As you say, we don't know them. This one's the son of an earl, I remember hearing his name before," Poppy said, accompanied by the shuffling of cards as she read them. "This one's name is familiar, something about a carriage race through Hyde Park..."

The maid entered again. "Excuse me, miss."

"What's the matter?" Rose asked. "Is one of them not taking no for an answer?" Sometimes gentlemen got upset when others were not at home to them, taking it as a personal affront.

"Oh, no, miss. They all left immediately. But this just arrived for you." The maid carefully placed a box in Rose's lap.

Rosalind felt along the edge and opened the box. The decadent smell of chocolate floated into the room. "Oh, that's divine," she said. She loved good food; she had practically lived in the kitchens as a child.

"Is there a note?" Poppy asked, coming over. She must have seen nothing, for she said, "That's odd. First a phalanx of would-be suitors, and now an anonymous gift!"

"Perhaps Lady Herbert sent it, as a sort of apology for what happened on the dance floor last night." Not that the hostess was too blame for her guest's bad behavior.

"No, I don't think so," Poppy disagreed. "She did send round a note earlier—I should have said, but I got distracted with all the callers. She expressed deep horror that such a trick was played, and she promised to not invite Hynes to any of her future events until he learned his lesson."

"Hmm." Rose wondered what would constitute "learning his lesson." Hynes was a member of the gentry and quite wealthy, according to what she'd learned. Such men always seemed to be forgiven for their transgressions, no matter how shocking. Even Viscount Norbury, who was scandal personified, was welcome anywhere he chose to go. How much of that was due to his personal charm (admittedly a strong force), and how much was simply because he was a man with a title? Rose didn't like to think about it.

The bell rang again.

"Oh, what now?" Grumbling, Alice turned and went to find out who was at the door. She returned a moment later, with someone in tow.

"My goodness, it's Lord Norbury," Poppy declared loudly, mostly to let Rose know what was happening. "Odd that you should arrive just after we instructed the servants to inform everyone we are not at home."

"He said it was very important, miss," Alice said hastily.

"That we shall discover," Poppy said. "That will be all, Alice. And we are not at home to anyone else, understand?"

"Yes, miss." Alice's footsteps pattered into the back of the house.

"Miss Blake," Adrian addressed Rosalind as he approached where she was sitting, "did you not tell your companion that I had plans to call on you?"

"You must forgive me, my lord, for not believing everything you say." Rosalind strove to keep her voice cool, but couldn't help smiling.

"You would not be the first, Miss Blake."

"So we have heard," Poppy said, so softly that Rose almost missed it.

"If I may," he said, returning his attention to Rosalind. "Hold out your hands?"

She did, and he placed a single stem into them. "A rose?" she asked, inhaling a whiff of rich scent.

"Just a token I thought you might enjoy, seeing as it is your namesake." He sat down on a chair opposite Rosalind. The faint smell of sandalwood drifted toward her. Perhaps that was the scent of his soap.

"I appreciate the thought, my lord," Rose said, holding the flower out to Poppy in a wordless request to find a vessel for it so it would not wilt, "but why did you think it necessary?"

"I do unnecessary things all the time," he returned. "It's the necessary ones I tend to neglect. But in your case, I have not. It was necessary to see you again."

Rosalind's heart beat a little faster. "Why?"

"I wanted to verify that you were not an apparition. Someone so lovely as you shouldn't really be allowed out in London. There are too many predators around."

"I have heard that, sir. I've also heard they can take many forms, not all of them unpleasant."

"You are right, Miss Blake. Not every suit of armor contains a knight. Some are quite empty."

"And, of course, it is not only knights who are chivalrous," Rose added quietly. "I would rather judge a man by his deeds than his title."

"Your lack of sight has not affected your perception, Miss Blake. But this brings me to another question. You told me last night that you have no suitors, yet today you mentioned a number of callers. So what am I to believe? How many suitors do you currently have?"

"My lord?" she asked, puzzled.

"Is the number too high to conveniently count?"

"A few days ago, I would have said that the number

takes no time at all to count," she responded faintly. "Though I seem to have attracted more attention. I do not know why, but today I was beset by callers for some reason."

"Let us agree that it is because you deserve to be admired." Lord Norbury stood up then. "Well, I have taken up more than enough of your time. I am delighted that Hynes's stupid prank has done no lasting evil to you. I wish you good day, my fair lady. I hope this meeting is not our last." He bent and captured Rose's hand, kissing it gently.

Across the room, Poppy cleared her throat meaningfully. Norbury laughed softly as he straightened up. "And a good day to you as well, Miss St. George. You will, I have no doubt, continue to protect my lady as you have so far."

"Against all threats," Poppy agreed, a hint of steel in her tone.

But Norbury merely said, "Miss Blake is lucky to have you as a friend. I would suggest that you take special care about these new callers. Some, like Hynes last night, might not have the best of intentions."

"But you do?" Poppy asked, very boldly.

"When it comes to Miss Blake, believe me, I want no harm to come to her."

Poppy paused, then said, in what Rose recognized as her "thoughtful" tone, "Very well, my lord. Thank you for the advice."

"Thank you for accepting it in the spirit it is meant. I will make my exit while there is still time." He left the house without further ado.

His timing proved apt, for Mrs. Blake was set to return within a quarter hour.

Poppy let her breath out with a whoosh. "Rose, what

are we going to do?"

"About what?"

"Lord Norbury!"

"What needs to be done?" Rosalind tipped her head to one side, considering. "He was polite to stop by. But do you really think he'll become a fixture in my life?"

"He asked if you had suitors."

"I suspect that he asks all sorts of awkward questions just to needle people. One can tell he likes making others squirm." She had almost squirmed when she felt his lips on her hand. Like his caress the previous night, it probably appeared quite proper. But there was a hidden sensuality about it that was deliberate, meant for her alone to notice.

"What color is the rose?" she asked, mostly to distract Poppy from the current topic.

"Pale pink. It's very lovely," she added grudgingly. "I put it in a drinking glass, but I'll ask Alice to find a proper vase for it."

By luck and determination, the girls kept news of the visit from Mrs. Blake, instead chattering about the unexpected cavalcade of surprise visitors. Rosalind was in a strange mood for the rest of the day, however, even as she attempted to remind herself that Lord Norbury was merely being polite in calling on her after a dance, and probably just being funny when he asked how many suitors she had. But then, there was the kiss in the garden last night. Could he possibly actually be interested in her?

Late in the afternoon, she sat in the window of her bedroom, basking in the warmth of the afternoon sun and the mellow sounds of spring. Taking a bonbon from the little box—which Poppy had quickly hidden before her mother might see it—Rosalind bit into the chocolate, savoring the smell and taste of it. The center was laced with brandy, and she breathed in slowly, taking in the flavors.

Who would have sent such a gift? It was perfect, really, a gift that Rose could truly enjoy.

Then she laughed softly, licking her lips. It had to be Norbury. Why was she surprised? A rake like him must know very well what women enjoyed.

Chapter 5

AFTER CALLING ON ROSE, ADRIAN was too restless to go home, so he went to his usual fencing *salle* to practice. There, his instructor, Salvator Caizo, conducted a series of excruciating sequences that had Adrian almost begging for mercy. Almost. He was too much of a competitor to ever admit he was ready to drop.

By the end of the afternoon session, he was sweating, breathing hard, and he wanted to rip his clothes off (he didn't object to being in such a state, but there were other, more pleasant ways to get there). Adrian nevertheless steadied himself, preparing for another sequence. "En garde," he told his teacher.

Caizo waved him off. "Enough. An exhausted mind retains little of what it learns. Put away the foil and drink some fresh water."

Adrian gratefully headed toward a wooden stand where a dozen swords were kept, carefully putting his back among them.

"I heard you had a duel recently," Caizo mentioned then. "But you chose pistols. That's what happens when you skip practice!"

"Not at all, Maestro. If I chose swords, I would have sliced him to ribbons. The man was too inept to lose a proper fencing bout without damage. Whereas with a pistol, I simply aim to the left, miss him by a mile, and the demands of honor are met."

"Ah, that makes sense. But a pity all the same. Guns have no elegance, no heritage. Any man can pick up a gun and fire it."

"I believe that's the goal." Adrian had once harbored a desire to join the army, drawn to the image of glorious battle and serving bravely and all the sorts of things young boys believed. His father roundly refused to pay for a commission and his mother told Adrian that she'd throw herself into the sea if he ever put on a uniform.

It wasn't until he was older that he learned that his own father's poor health had been the result of a campaign in the American wilderness during hostilities between the British forces and an upstart bunch of colonists. He'd been shot, suffering a punctured lung at the tender age of eighteen. He'd lived (surprising everyone but his fiancée back home). However, he'd never been fully healthy since then, and when a particularly nasty winter brought pneumonia to his lungs, he couldn't fight it off. He'd grown thinner and weaker, until he was just a shadow of himself, an old man in a massive bed. Adrian visited him every day, listening to his father's whispered words, but at the end, he'd actually grown scared of his father's form. Was it possible that such a strong man could be reduced to this? Was this the fate of everyone?

Perhaps that revelation was part of what spurred Adrian to his hedonistic ways. After all, his bad behavior started not long before his father's death. He'd left childhood behind and plunged directly into a very adult world. And for the most part, he had survived it.

Adrian returned home to bathe and dress for the evening, though he found himself strangely at loose ends

—London offered a buffet of amusements for gentleman who could pay, and Adrian couldn't think of a single one that appealed to him at the moment.

So he made his way to his favorite club, not having made any decision about how he ought to spend the rest of his evening. He had time. Like many gentlemen of his class, Adrian considered the social "evening" to last until dawn streaked the sky.

At the club, he slid into a comfortable chair near one of the fireplaces, and sipped a very fine brandy while he stared into the flames. As Adrian was known to be prone to bouts of moodiness, not a single man there would have thought his introspection odd. But in fact, he was thinking along very different lines than usual. Lines of thought that were heavily colored with rose...

Later, perhaps three brandies later, a voice broke into his musings. "Norbury, are you plotting something really nefarious?"

At that question, Adrian looked up from his seat at the club to see none other than Carlos de la Guerra looming over him, which Carlos could only do because Adrian was sitting—he was a good three inches taller than his friend. Unusually, Carlos wasn't smiling. Instead, his normally merry brown eyes held a spark of concern.

"What gives you that idea?" Adrian asked. "And what took you so long to get here?" Carlos usually dropped by the club earlier, knowing Adrian often hid out there when the social demands of London became too annoying, which was to say nearly every evening.

Carlos replied, "I'm late getting here because I've been getting stopped left and right by men wanting to know the latest about you, which of course they assume I'm privy to."

That was a fair assumption, because Carlos was probably Adrian's closest friend. It was an odd pairing, to be sure. Adrian was a son of aristocracy and close to the cream of English society. Carlos was…not. He was well-born in his way, the child of wealthy landowners near Santo Domingo on the Caribbean island of Hispaniola. After all, the two had met at Eton. He was educated and skilled, as likely to be reading a book or sailing his own ship to ports on his family's business.

However, Adrian happened to know that the de la Guerra family business was only partially legitimate. Yes, they were importers and exporters of goods. Santo Domingo relied upon importation to supply many things the islanders simply could not produce on their own. And in turn the de la Guerra family fleet loaded up what Santo Domingo did produce, namely tobacco and beef, and sold it in European ports.

What *also* got bought and sold in those parts was none of Adrian's business. Carlos often hinted that he knew far more about the smuggling trade than any upright citizen should. But as Adrian didn't rely on taxes on goods for his income, he didn't care at all if smuggling was alive and active on the English coast. As long as Carlos watched his back and didn't get himself killed, all was well.

"There's been chatter tonight of you pursuing some sweet little deaf maiden. I thought it sounded like a lot of nonsense. Didn't you just duel against the Earl of Tindell over a few indiscreet letters?"

Adrian waved a hand to indicate his disdain. "The affair with Victoria ended two years ago. Unfortunately, it seems a spiteful servant just happened to find some of my letters to her, and just happened to moved them to Tindell's study, who just happened to be already irate about his dwindling finances. Sometimes a man loses his sense of proportion, and Tindell dealt with his problems by insisting on fighting with me. A matter of honor, as he put it. I chose pistols to keep things simple."

"So you deliberately missed him? Good," Carlos said, sitting down across from his friend.

"I think he was so happy to not be dead at the end of the duel that he'll be content to live quietly for a while." Adrian paused, reflecting. "In all honesty, I've been mostly respectable for years now."

"Yes, but everyone still recalls your past. Anyway, I'm glad you're not dallying with debutantes fresh from the schoolroom."

"She's a couple years out of the schoolroom," Adrian said thoughtlessly.

"Then there *is* a deaf maiden?" Carlos put his drink down, his expression alarmed.

"Miss Blake is blind, not deaf."

"Wait, you really are seducing a virgin?"

Adrian glared at him. "The *ton* must be completely starved for gossip if this rates as a scandal. I met her by chance yesterday, and quite liked her. But it was only a dance. I'll probably never even see her again." Except that he'd called on her once, and already told her he'd call on her again...twice more than he usually allotted for misses on the marriage mart.

"Well, glad it's just a rumor, especially after...well, let's not get into it. Now come on. I've had a hankering for a game of cards."

Adrian and Carlos left the club, searching out livelier entertainment. They found the card games they sought, amid the gaming hells that offered gamblers every game of chance imaginable, from a simple round of *vingt-et-un* to wagers on the latest boxing matches, cockfights, and more obscure bets. Adrian once saw a pool on when the Theatre Royal would catch on fire next. Some men would gamble on anything.

He preferred cards, and so did Carlos. They spent a few hours at the tables, Adrian losing a little and not minding it at all. His family had enough money that he rarely thought about money, truly an indicator of his lucky position in life. Carlos won a little and looked quite pleased about it.

Just after Carlos suggested they head out before his wins turned to losses, Adrian was distracted by something over near the betting books. Did someone just say the name *Rosalind*?

"Come with me," Adrian muttered to his friend.

"What is it?"

"Probably nothing. I just want to see the latest wagers. Looks like something's got those men excited."

As they drew closer, Adrian heard the name again. Surely this was a coincidence, because he'd met a girl with that name and was inclined to hear it everywhere.

"I bet I could do it in five days," one man was saying to his companion.

"That's too fast, unless there's kidnapping involved. Think of it! The parents, the house, the need to be polite for a while…"

"A week, then." The first man raised his voice and told the person writing in the betting book. "Put me down for a week. Ten pounds."

"What's this?" Carlos asked the pair of men in a mild, interested tone. Adrian hung back, and the other men did not notice him standing there.

"New game!" the first man said eagerly, the mad light of the inveterate gambler in his eyes. "All the rage. Seduce a virgin."

"That's the oldest game," Carlos retorted instantly.

"There's a twist. It's a particular virgin—Miss Rosalie

Baker or something like that. She's blind—raises the challenge because you have to get past the chaperones and whatnot. Pool starts at three days from meeting her to ruining her, which seems a bit rushed, all the way out to a month…which might as well be ordinary courtship at that point." The man seemed utterly unaware of Carlos's appalled expression, and he still did not notice Adrian, which was good, because Adrian was livid.

"Why her?" Carlos asked, obviously trying to keep his voice in check.

The other men shrugged. "Who knows? It's got to be someone, so we can have a wager. Why not her?"

Adrian, his jaw clenched, took a few steps back, and Carlos swiftly withdrew as well, steering Adrian toward the doors.

The pair headed outside, before violence broke out.

"This is my fault," Adrian said in a low voice, once they were walking down the narrow street, Adrian's steps so fast that Carlos had to hurry to keep pace.

"You don't know that," his friend said.

"What else could I think? I just met the girl. I had *half* a dance with her, and because I am who I am, everyone assumes it's a new game, to ruin a virgin for fun?"

"This may blow over in a day or two. After all, how many men are actually going to place a wager on such a thing?" Then Carlos winced and seemed to hear his own words. "Never mind. We're in London. There will be more than enough men eager to gamble on someone else's misfortune."

"Exactly."

"Though perhaps by tomorrow, another ridiculous wager will gain the attention of the gamblers. That's really what we should hope for. Want me to challenge one of these British ship captains to some sort of race down the

Thames?" Carlos had ready access to his family's ships, and though he did not look it, he was a skilled sailor and helmsman.

"How will that help? The bets on Miss Blake have already been placed." That was the problem, for wagers could not be rescinded.

"What else do you recommend? You can't exactly stand guard over her, can you? For one thing it's impractical. For another, you're the last person who should be seen around her if the goal is to *save* her reputation."

Adrian glared at him, but Carlos held firm. "What? It's true. If I were a father, and thank the Lord I'm not, I wouldn't let a daughter within half a mile of you."

"Thank you for that."

"You know I'm right."

"Yes, and that's why I want to clock you," Adrian muttered. "I don't suppose you could get the whole Blake family on your ship and sail them to some secluded cove until this nonsense ends?"

"Could, but I won't. We've got very firm rules about hauling human cargo. We're not Saint-Domingue," he added with disdain. The neighboring province held a much, much higher number of slaves, which was a point of frequent contention on the already contentious island.

"Then another plan is required," Adrian said quietly.

"What are you going to do? You've got that look in your eye," Carlos noted. "Which usually heralds chaos."

"Not sure yet. I'll sleep on it. But one thing is certain. I'm not letting half a dance be the cause of that girl's ruin. Any man aiming to destroy her reputation will regret it. If I have to fight all of them off with a sword, I'll do it."

"Lord Norbury, knight errant!" Carlos said with a laugh. "Who would believe it?"

"No one," he agreed. "Which is my advantage."

Chapter 6

❀ ⚬ ❀

THE NEXT DAY, ROSE WAS in the morning room, practicing a new piece on the piano. Rose practiced diligently, since music was something she not only excelled at, but loved. Knowing that she would be occupied for quite a while, Poppy and her mother always used the mornings to run errands or go out visiting, allowing Rose to practice what she'd learned in her lesson the previous day.

She was so intent on learning the piece that she jumped when she felt a hand on her shoulder.

"Good afternoon, Miss Blake," a cheerful voice sounded in her ears.

"Why, Mr. Evans!" she said, recognizing his voice. She twisted around on the bench, wondering if the maid had entered the room as well. She couldn't hear any other person. "How did you get in here?"

"The maid let me in. I told her not to announce me, as you should not be distracted from your practice. You really are accomplished," he added.

"Thank you. I'm still learning this piece, and I don't usually play for strangers until they're perfected."

"Well, it's a good thing I'm no stranger. Have you been outside yet? It's a perfect day for a ride."

"I'm sorry to say I cannot join you, Mr. Evans. Both Poppy and my mother are away at the moment."

"Which is just as well!" Evans said with a laugh. "You don't need a chaperone for a ride around the park."

"Don't I?" Rose asked. Most people, even the stuffiest matrons, would admit that a single woman could ride alone with a man as long as they stayed in public view. She also knew that she would be held to stricter standards due to her handicap. But she did want to go out. It was so difficult to remain confined, knowing that others were able to do whatever they liked.

"You certainly don't. Besides, it will be fun." Evans walked over to the mantel and yanked the bell pull, the sound jangling in the servants' quarters, barely audible to Rose's ears.

Alice appeared moments later. "Yes, sir?" she asked, realizing that it was the guest who had summoned her, as Rose was still seated at the piano.

"Miss Blake is accompanying me on a brief ride. Will you fetch her a bonnet?" Perhaps it was his mere expectation of being obeyed, but Alice murmured assent and walked out.

"Interesting," Rosalind commented, impressed by the maid's instant capitulation. Then she heard Mr. Evans step toward her, his mass reducing the light from the windows as he leaned over her. His hand enveloped her own.

"Come," he said. She rose and allowed him to escort her out of the room, barely able to grab her walking stick, which had been leaning in its place against the side of the piano.

In the hall, Alice was waiting.

"Your Pamela hat, miss," she said, touching Rose's hand and exchanging the stick for the hat.

Rosalind took the large hat that she'd got for that

spring, having been informed that it was the height of fashion (especially after Poppy acquired a few yards of silk ribbon and added it to the hat). She tied the buttery-soft ribbon under her chin and told the maid to inform her mother and Poppy where she was, if they should return before she did. Alice handed over the walking stick again, since Rose did not like to leave home without it, even though it was unlikely to be needed for a ride in a carriage.

And then they were outside, with the sun-warmed air all around.

Mr. Evans helped her into the open coach.

"All ready?" he asked.

"I think so," she said, but was still surprised by the sudden lurch forward as the horses began to walk. Evans steadied her by gripping her elbow with one hand while he drove. "I'm used to a closed coach," she admitted.

"You'll soon get used to this," he assured her. "Shall I head to the river, or the promenade?"

"Oh, the promenade." Rosalind settled back to enjoy the ride. The sounds of the city of London surrounded her: the calls of people, the clip-clop of horses, the bark of street vendors and children. The smell of blossoming trees filled the air, and Rose inhaled happily when they passed a row of apple trees.

They rode down the promenade, Mr. Evans calling out loud and cheerful greetings to several people that he passed. They chatted of inconsequential things, and Rose found herself enjoying the ride (perhaps more than she enjoyed her companion, who was not exactly a sparkling conversationalist).

Moving though the park, the sounds of other people growing fainter as Evans chose a less-traveled track. "Much prettier on these side paths, isn't it?" he asked with no apparent recognition that Rose was not in a position to judge.

They continued on for a short while, and then Evans muttered something too low for her to hear.

The carriage lurched to a halt, nearly sending Rose to the floor as she was pitched forward.

"My word, what was that?" she gasped.

"That's unfortunate," said Mr. Evans, not sounding very upset. "Hold one moment, and I'll go see what's the matter."

The balance of the carriage shifted as he leapt down to the ground. Rose heard footsteps circle the carriage and then heard the whinny of the horses.

"What happened?" she asked when he returned.

"Patch of mud," he explained. "Looks like the wheel got sunk and hit a rock. I'm afraid the wheel is damaged."

Rose thought he sounded quite calm about it, so she assumed it was a minor issue. She asked, "Then shall we walk to the street that borders the park so we can hail a ride to return me home?"

"Oh, no, much too far! We'll wait here for rescue." He returned to the carriage, the springs of the seat squeaking as he slid onto it.

"Rescue?" she echoed.

"Bound to be someone by in a little bit," he told her cheerfully.

"Where in the park are we?" she asked. Rose only knew the family's usual route, because Mr. Blake did not vary in his habits. She tipped her head, listening closely. She heard the rustle of early leaves, and the chirping of a hundred birds, and even the rush of a small brook somewhere nearby. But no people. No distant conversations, or the clop of hooves indicating a rider passing or a carriage along the path behind them. "It seems quite isolated."

"Nonsense. Won't be more than a quarter hour, I'm sure. Maybe half an hour."

Where in London's most popular park could they be that it would take so long to even be seen, let alone for someone to notice that the carriage was incapacitated? Rose began to feel uneasy.

"I should prefer that we walk to get help," she said, reaching for her walking stick, and finding a little comfort when she gripped the cool silver top.

"You're not wearing shoes for walking," he pointed out, "and it is very muddy."

He moved closer to her, slipping an arm around her shoulders. "Don't worry, I'll ensure you're not bored."

His mouth descended on hers in a kiss that assumed far too much about her interest and her enthusiasm.

Rose pushed him away. "Sir! You mistake me."

"Do I?" he asked. "You seemed quite happy to come along, not having the slightest idea where I'd take you."

"You implied you'd keep to the main paths!"

"Well, what else would I say?" He leaned over Rose again, pushing her back in the seat as he pressed himself against her, his hands hot on her chest and arms pawing.

"Get off me!" Rose protested, trying to squirm away.

"Enjoy it," he told her, ignoring her attempts to escape. "A blind girl can't be too choosy about who she asks to seduce her."

"I did not ask for anything!" she hissed, offended and frankly scared now. "Let me out of here or I shall scream."

"Do that," he said. "I'd love it. Everyone comes running, and sees you all ravished and panting…"

"Ugh!" Rose hated the image he described. She twisted away from him, reaching for the door with the flat of her hand, finding the handle a moment later. Just then, she realized the walking stick was still in the carriage. Drat. Well, she'd run on her own, even if she fell or tripped over a tree root or made a mess of herself. Anything was better than staying with this horrid excuse for a man.

Once on the ground, Rose started walking away from the carriage, not much caring where she was headed. She held her arms out in front of her. Now she was probably going to run smack into a tree, completing her humiliation.

Just then, she did step directly into something, but not a tree. It was a person, the body solid and strong and unmoving. Hands reached up to hold her, and a familiar voice said, "Miss Blake, it seems I am always finding you inexplicably solo."

After a beat of total shock, Rose allowed herself to accept the truth. Adrian Marsh was there, just when she needed him.

"Oh, my lord," she gasped, not entirely clear in her own mind whether the words were a prayer of thanks or simply polite address. Did it matter?

"Steady, Rose," he murmured, softly enough that only she heard it. "I'll sort this out."

Louder, he spoke to the suitor who had proven so unsuitable. "Good day, Mr. Evans. It *is* Evans, isn't it?"

Evans sounded startled, and not happy about a rescuer appearing. "Yes, that is my name, though we have not met, sir."

"Well, that's a mercy," Norbury said dryly, allowing the other man to hear his comment. "An odd place to stop a carriage, and with such a charming passenger in need of especially careful handling, I must note."

While he spoke, he kept Rose close to him, his arm around her shoulders in a protective embrace. She leaned into him while listening to the exchange, hearing new levels of animosity growing with every word.

"The carriage wheel is damaged," Mr. Evans replied, his tone sullen and combative—but not *too* combative. He sounded like a man who knew how this particular battle would end.

"Sloppy," Adrian commented, his voice like steel. "The wheel looks fine to me."

"Well, it isn't," Evans snapped.

"My lord," Rose began to say, thinking that she'd need to exonerate herself. "I…"

"Why, of course I'll escort you home," Adrian said, as if that was what she'd asked. "As it happens, my curricle has perfectly fine wheels, and plenty of room for such a light burden as yourself. Evans here can deal with *his* mess however he likes."

Adrian must have sensed her trembling, because he put one hand at her back as he turned her away from Evans and toward his own conveyance.

"Wait," she blurted out. "My walking stick—he's got it."

"Stay there." Adrian left her, did something that caused Evans to yelp in protest, and a moment later he returned, handing her the stick.

"Oh, thank you," she breathed.

"This way, Miss Blake."

Rose heard the nicker of the horses as they approached—she'd been so upset before that she hadn't even heard them come up. Adrian helped her in with steady hands, and he went round the other side to climb in himself.

Rosalind had never been in such a vehicle before, and felt it was almost like riding on nothing at all. Unlike a coach, there was no sense of enclosure. The little curricle was light and let the world in. The seat moved as Adrian got in beside her. She heard him pick up the reins, eager to be off.

"Quite secure, Miss Blake?"

"Yes, thank you." Was she secure? In a physical sense, she was better off than she was a moment ago. But who would have thought that she'd be safer with a known libertine than a respectable gentleman?

Chapter 7

❦

"HOLD ON," ADRIAN TOLD ROSE. "We'll be moving… now."

The horses reacted to his command, and the curricle rolled forward, slowly at first, and then with increasing speed.

"His wheel wasn't broken, was it?" she asked when she could no longer keep silent.

"No, it was not," Adrian said tightly.

"And you knew exactly what he was about, even though you pretended otherwise."

"It was not subtle," he agreed. "But since he did want me to react a certain way, it pleased me to take another tack to frustrate him. I do enjoy frustrating toad eaters like him."

"I hope I never hear his voice again," Rose said.

"He'd be an idiot to call upon you after this, but I'll drop a word to your parents so they can make it clear to the household that you'll never be home to him."

"It was as if he wanted to get caught with me!" she said, disgusted at the memory. "Why would he do that?"

"Best not to speculate on the motives of a fool, Miss Blake. But in the future, you will have to be much more careful with gentlemen you do not know."

"What would I have done if you'd not happened by?" Rose turned to him. "It seems more than chance."

He chuckled and said easily, "Well, as it happens, I was heading to your home. I wanted to offer you a ride through the park, and lo, here we are riding through the park."

"That makes it twice you have rescued me from the ill intentions of other men. I fear, my lord, that as a rakehell, you are not living up to expectations."

He laughed, and said, "Well, I am rather contrarian. Always have been."

"Is that true? What was your first contrary act?"

"Well, I suppose it was the act of being born at all. I was not expected to survive, and my mother told me that every midwife and doctor said there was no hope. But I never liked to listen to others, so I did live that first night, and persisted in living ever since. My mother said every day with me was a miracle...which is the sort of thing a mother would say, yes?"

"I should hope so. My own mother tends to say things like *Rose, stay out of the sun*, and *Rose, stay away from the window, you'll catch cold*. But she says them out of love," Rose added loyally.

He didn't speak for a few moments, and Rosalind understood that he was negotiating the more crowded pathways of the park. But then he lightly touched her hand, as if to remind her who she was with. "What are you thinking of?"

"I was thinking that today was the first time in years that I've been outside the house with someone who was not a member of my family, and now I've ridden with not one man, but two. Mama will probably lock me up once she hears what happened."

"Is that true?" He sounded surprised by that. "Because you are a woman, or because you cannot see?"

His bluntness didn't upset Rosalind. "Both, I suppose. My mother thinks me very fragile."

"You are her only daughter, are you not? She feels responsible for you."

"She has difficulty understanding that I am not still twelve years old." Rosalind sighed. "Forgive me, I shouldn't talk like this." She could smell the clean spring air, and knew that they must have returned to the main roads of the promenade. However, this time she felt no fear. She trusted Lord Norbury's judgment on where to drive. "Please tell me what's going on in the park."

"The usual," Adrian noted, probably looking around with a disinterested air. "Lots of carriages and riders. The latest frocks, and pearls on every limb. The polite society are out, parading for all to see. Those with things to sell are selling them as best they can: their jewels and titles and offspring." His voice grew increasingly bitter as he spoke.

"You don't think much of them," Rosalind said calmly.

He replied, "I'm nodding in complete agreement, so you know. I don't think much of them, but perhaps only because they don't think much of me."

"Why not?"

He paused, then said, "Why not? A thousand reasons, some of them totally unsuitable to mention in mixed company. In short, I have created a reputation for myself."

"As a rake." Rosalind didn't see any point in concealing her knowledge. "I have heard about you. But in any case, it doesn't explain why you so hate society."

"I don't like their rules. Nor do I play by them. Society loathes nothing more than someone who doesn't kowtow to their rituals. They'd push that person to the edge if they could, to the demimonde. But no one can push me out. Hard to tell a viscount what to do."

"Yes, you are still invited to the beaumonde's parties," she said.

"Rake or not, I'm still wealthy." He shrugged. "And they're avaricious."

"You're cynical."

"Yes," he agreed shortly. "As well as being an unpleasant conversationalist. I apologize."

"Not at all. I'm delighted when people speak honestly to me. It hardly ever happens—except with Poppy."

"You're lucky to have a friend like Miss St. George."

"I am indeed." Rosalind smiled, thinking of her. "I would trust her with my life. I don't know what will happen when..." She trailed off.

"When what?"

"Poppy has turned down offers of marriage already. But she's a remarkable person, and I know that she will be married someday. I shall have to find a new companion when she leaves our home, a paid one most likely. It won't be the same."

"But you might marry before her. You are also a remarkable person."

Rosalind blushed at his words. "Your opinion is, alas, not common. I am aware that I do not have the makings of a wife."

"No? I doubt that. I should think you do have the makings of a lover, or a muse."

"My lord," Rosalind began tartly, intent on reprimanding him. "That...was one of the nicest things anyone has ever told me." *Hmm*, she thought. *That reprimand lacked punch.*

Unexpectedly, he laughed. "I can see I'll have to work

much harder to shock you, Miss Blake."

They talked over many things during the course of the ride, which lasted longer than most, not that Rose noticed. Norbury did succeed in shocking her a few times, but she more than paid him back with an honesty he said he'd never before encountered from a woman.

Rosalind, for her part, delighted in their conversation, recognizing when Lord Norbury teased her, and occasionally tempted her with his words. With every passing minute, she understood more clearly why women fell for him against all advice. He did a truly shocking thing: he listened.

At one point he asked what Rose liked to do with her days, aside from music.

"I do nothing, really," she replied. "I mean, ladies don't do much in the first place. Our role is to visit each other's houses and eat exactly one teacake whilst gossiping about the latest style of neckline. But I do even less than that. I just…take what comes to me."

"Rosalind," he said, boldly using her first name, "that's the first time you've ever lied to me."

"Lied?" she echoed, horrified at his words. "What do you mean?"

"You paint yourself as passive, as someone without drive. But that is utter bullocks. You have taught yourself how to navigate a world you can no longer see, you study music, and you are quite capable of telling idiots to go to hell. In a drawing room boxing match, I'd bet on you over anyone else."

She laughed at the notion of ladies boxing over tea in a drawing room, but said, "It's kind of you to say that, but the fact of the matter is that I am heavily reliant on others for the most basic tasks."

"Everyone is," he argued. "I can't even get dressed in

the mornings without my valet. To say nothing of how I'd starve before I managed a proper breakfast."

"That's different."

"It's not so different. We are social animals, dependent on others for our survival. Some pretend otherwise, but they are only indulging in their own delusion. For if they were truly independent of society, why do they constantly show up in my club and try to win general approval for their declamations of how they don't desire to win approval?"

"Do they really?"

"Yes, just as you know ladies who gossip about not gossiping. It's human."

"A bit depressing, my lord."

"Realistic, that's all." He paused. "Should I stop talking? I've already burned your ears with words you're not supposed to know, not to mention excoriated the very society that has placed me in a position of wealth and comfort."

"I like it when you talk, actually," Rose confessed. "You're different than I thought you'd be."

"What did you think I'd be?"

"I'm not sure. More arrogant. More…flirtatious."

"Well, I am arrogant, and I would flirt with you if I thought I could get away with it."

"I think you know you *could* get away with it, and therefore you're restraining yourself. What would you do if you were unrestrained, I wonder."

"For starters, I'd spirit you away to a secret location."

"Obviously," she agreed. "It seems the standard practice. What then?"

"I'd seduce you in stages, naturally. I don't like to rush things."

"Not rush things? My lord, need I remind you that you

kissed me within a quarter hour of meeting me!"

"Yes, well, that was unplanned. In fact, one could argue that you seduced me that time...after all, what defenses did I have prepared against your onslaught of innocence?"

"That is a nonsensical phrase."

"True, though. If you'd been *trying* for a kiss from a scandalous rake, I wouldn't have been nearly so intrigued. Instead you asked for nothing, and therefore I simply had to plant a kiss on your pretty mouth. And of course, in my planned seduction, there will be more kissing."

"You are a fiend, sir," Rose said with a light laugh, though her stomach had decided to flip over at the memory of that kiss in the garden. "You are seducing me by merely outlining a plan of seduction. In full daylight, in public, in view of who knows how many citizens of London."

"Yes, I hoped you'd like it," he said with a sly warmth that nearly made her break out her fan.

"You shall need to talk about something extremely dull before you can return me to my house," she warned, knowing that she was in enough of a state of agitation that Poppy would immediately know something had occurred...even though nothing did.

Obligingly, Lord Norbury talked about his best friend's life in the colony of Santo Domingo, and how he'd come to England after the French took possession of most of the island of Hispaniola following the latest war, in which the Spanish had suffered significant losses.

The topic wasn't dull at all, but it was different enough that Rose was able to put aside her body's reactions to Adrian's previous discussion and settle on the carriage seat listening to stories set an ocean away.

"Why would anyone come to England after all that?"

she asked finally, thinking that London must seem very staid and boring.

"His family has trade interests that span many countries, and he's here to solidify some of them with British firms."

"Will he go back home, then?" Rose asked.

"Eventually, for a time. He doesn't seem likely to ever settle down anywhere, unless he gets the revolution he's been hoping for."

"Excuse me?" Rose asked, assuming she'd misheard.

"There are factions in Santo Domingo that chafe against being ruled from abroad. They'd prefer to rule themselves."

"Oh, like the States."

"Exactly. One would almost think that people prefer independence to the glorious honor of being ruled—and taxed—by His Majesty."

"Is that so, *my lord*?"

He laughed, acknowledging her point. "Yes, it must sound like nonsense coming from me. As a viscount, I benefit from the current order of things. I can't deny it. But being friends with Carlos has opened my eyes to a lot of things…er, pardon the expression."

Rose waved a hand to dismiss the notion that she was offended. "A figure of speech that arose because it is true. Vision is the most important sense. I don't expect the English language to change to accommodate my particular condition."

"Do you really think that? That vision is the most important sense?"

"Well, perhaps it is better to say that society considers it so. I can say that losing it has had rather a strong impact on me," Rose told him. "Losing my sense of smell would not be nearly so disruptive…only sad that I could not enjoy flowers and foods so much."

"What about hearing? If you lost that, you couldn't enjoy music."

"That's true," Rose said, struck. "I'd be devastated if I couldn't hear music or know what notes my fingers played on the pianoforte. It might be easier to navigate the world—a little—but for me, I think it *would* be worse to never hear again."

"For instance, you'd be denied the sound of my delightful conversation," Norbury noted wryly.

"Truly a horror to contemplate," Rose agreed, recognizing that he was returning the discussion to a lighter mood, keeping her from dwelling on thoughts that might sadden her.

This whole carriage ride had been a revelation. For a so-called rake, Adrian Marsh had behaved very properly…mostly. He had not once attempted to kiss her or push for any physical familiarities that the other man had been so quick to try. Part of Rose was relieved—she didn't want to have to fend off every single man who came within three feet of her. And of course, they were very much in public now, with the sounds of the city all around them, and many observers to passively chaperone by simply existing. But another part of her was a little saddened. It had been so exciting when he had flirted with her before. But he must have decided that there was no point in continuing to charm her so. It wasn't as if he was ever going to court Rose in a formal way. The scandalous Viscount Norbury wasn't going to settle down with a wallflower wife!

"I should return you to your home eventually," he said then. "I've pressed my luck very far already."

"Oh, but you rescued me, and that will go very far in addressing any concerns of my parents about how long

I've been out."

"Let us hope that's the case," Norbury said, not as optimistic.

In her driveway, he alighted quickly, but before he could get around to the other side of the curricle, a young boy hurried up and called to Rose. "I'm supposed to take you inside immediately, miss!"

"Yes, Jack," she said with a sigh. So she had been out too long. Her parents were back home and furious at her independence.

Norbury opened the door and helped her out, providing a very stable support, not to mention the gentle squeeze he gave her hand to offer her a bit of comfort.

"Do you want me to come in with you?" he asked. "To explain things?"

"I can manage," Rose said. "Though it is very kind of you to offer. And you know…I think it's best if neither of us mention Mr. Evans's behavior. After all, nothing actually happened, and if any hint were to get out…" She'd never be allowed past the threshold again. "I will find a discreet way to ensure Mr. Evans never troubles me again."

"Very well, Miss Blake. I will bow to your preference on this matter."

"Thank you," she breathed.

"But if you ever do need my assistance, whether regarding Evans or anything else, send word to me at Boodle's and I'll do whatever is needed."

"Let us hope it never gets so dire! My lord Norbury, I must thank you for a lovely afternoon. I do hope we will meet again."

"You may rely on it, Miss Blake," he promised. "Your walking stick."

She accepted it, and hurried inside, Jack hovering at

her elbow, telling her when she veered to one side.

In truth, Rose was confident of explaining the day's events to her parents, until she reached the drawing room, where it felt like she was walking into a winter storm. She heard the rustling skirts of Poppy and her mother. Her father crinkled his ever-present newspapers when she entered.

"There she is at last!" he cried with a false heartiness. Evidently, the household had been much more concerned than Rose thought, if her father was waiting at home.

"Where were you?" her mother hissed.

"As I'm sure Alice told you, I went for a ride in the park at the request of Mr. Evans," Rosalind admitted, aware that this innocent truth would be taken in the worst possible way.

"But you returned with Lord Norbury! What happened? Have you lost your mind?"

"No, just my sight," she retorted. She heard Poppy gasp, but it sounded suspiciously like the beginning of a laugh.

Mr. Blake was as appalled as her mother. "Rosie, darling, please explain!"

So Rose gave a much simplified version of events, not hinting at any impropriety on Evans's part.

"I wish you had not accepted the gentleman's invitation, Rose. It was far too impulsive. You could have destroyed your reputation and our family honor."

"By going for a ride?" Rosalind asked. "We were in the park the entire time. It's not as if I ran away with him to Gretna Green."

Her mother gasped again. "How dare you joke about it! And anyway, what had Norbury to do with all this?"

"Because Mr. Evans's carriage was damaged, and we had to stop. Lord Norbury came across us, and didn't think I should have to wait for Mr. Evans to repair the wheel, or whatever it was. He offered to escort me home himself, which was very chivalrous. But since it was so nice out, we took a slightly longer route through the promenade. Then he drove me home, and here I am before you, hale and whole."

"Rosalind, you are so innocent. I *know* what Mrs. Bloomfield told me when you were at school with her. And I have always tried to follow her advice to allow you space to make your own decisions, so that you may grow up and not be coddled like an infant. But you don't understand…"

"Oh, now I'm innocent? A moment ago you made it sound as if I were a barque of frailty."

"Guard your tongue!"

"Yes, Mother." (By rights, Rose should not be aware of this term for a prostitute, but Poppy had learned it and told Rose, who was so intrigued by the fanciful euphemism that she never forgot it.)

"Rosalind, dear," Mr. Blake began again, clearly keeping his voice in the range of calm. "We do not wish to hurt you. But I do not think you comprehend the gravity of the situation."

"I do not. Poppy has done exactly the same sort of thing on a number of occasions, and you never reacted like this."

"Poppy was escorted by respectable young men who were approved by us. Lord Norbury is neither respectable nor approved! And neither is Mr. Evans," he added, almost absently.

"Excuse me, Papa, but Lord Norbury behaved with perfect courtesy. Indeed, I am very lucky he happened by."

"I am relieved to hear it. But believe me, Rose," Mr.

Blake went on, "I know more about his past than you ever could. His reputation is of the worst kind. He has no respect for anything and regards women as..." Her mother coughed loudly. "Mere diversions," her father concluded lamely. "You could not know this, and I realize that he of course would keep you ignorant of his sins."

"I only wanted to enjoy myself," Rosalind said quietly. "I do not usually have the opportunity to do such a simple thing as a ride in the park."

Her mother sighed, now saddened. "I know, dear. Your lapse in judgment is understandable, and it seems that all is well. You are forgiven this time. But please consider your family's standing as well as your own desires. No more rides with gentlemen, and no more doing anything unsanctioned."

"Yes, Mama," she replied, chastened.

"Now go upstairs and rest. You looked flushed."

Upstairs, Poppy embraced her cousin. "I'm so sorry. When your mama looked out the window and saw it was Norbury's carriage, she nearly had a fit. What *really* happened with Mr. Evans? That was no full story you told."

"Evans's carriage wasn't in trouble," Rose said. "He drove me to a secluded place and stopped it deliberately so he could get me alone."

"That seems quick," Poppy muttered. "He just *met* you, and it's not as if you were wildly in love with him and hoping to be compromised."

"Eww," Rose said, wrinkling her nose. "No, and certainly I would not choose Mr. Evans for the honor. He was rather boorish."

"But Norbury was not?"

"He was a perfect gentleman, and I am grateful beyond words that he happened to pass by and rescue me."

"'Rescued by the Rake,'" Poppy said. "My goodness,

it sounds like a title of one of those dreadful stories in those dreadful journals."

"Snob," Rose accused. "And anyway, you love those journals." (Rose knew this to be true, since Poppy paid Alice to buy them for her, and she hid them under her bed, reading aloud to Rose on late nights when the girls didn't want to sleep.) "Mama is being quite overblown about all this. It was just a ride."

"I know. But, well, he *is* a rake."

Rosalind sighed." And now I'll not be able to talk to him ever again."

"I'm not so sure of that," Poppy murmured, squeezing her cousin's hand. "I don't think Norbury is the type who is easily discouraged."

Chapter 8

AFTER ADRIAN HAD RETURNED ROSE safely to the Blake house, he drove toward the park again. His expression was impassive, but he was furious. To think that if he'd chosen a slightly different route earlier, he'd never have noticed the carriage off the path, and not recognized the distinctive figure of Rose inside. Oh, Evans surely wanted to be caught with her...but *not* by Norbury.

Following the incident with Mr. Evans, Adrian realized that he'd have to be even more careful around Rose, and more diligent about assessing potential threats to her. He dispatched Carlos to a few gaming hells to learn what he could about the specific men making wagers on Rose. Carlos was the perfect man for such a job, and Adrian was confident that he'd return with a whole list of names.

As for Adrian himself, he had to figure out how he could stay close enough to Rose to protect her without adding fuel to the fire of the rumors. Which would be difficult.

Not that he anticipated any trouble getting into the Blake house. After all, he was a gentleman, and had (more or less) a proper acquaintance with all the ladies of the house. He hadn't actually planned on spending so much time with Rose today, wishing not to appear too attentive. For his solo ride in the curricle, he had dressed with his usual care, wearing a navy coat over a simple white shirt. His pants were as plain as possible. He disdained faddish colors and embellishments, considering them the purview of dandies. Happily, his curricle could easily accommodate one more, and he was glad that he looked as presentable as he did, taking Rose around the park in public view, mostly to establish that nothing scandalous could possibly be happening.

But that young Mr. Evans. What an ass. Adrian hoped Miss Poppy would be extra vigilant about letting other men (excluding Adrian) from dallying with Rose. But he didn't press the matter—Adrian didn't know what would happen if Poppy learned about the drunken bets in the gaming hell the other night, but he guessed it might be... loud. He did not want the young lady to take *any* action on Rose's part. She might do something everyone would regret.

Adrian drove back to his town house, hoping that Carlos would be there. His friend had rooms at one of London's finest hotels, but he also was a frequent guest at Adrian's home, and the servants had strict instructions to treat him as a resident. Adrian liked it when Carlos stayed at the house, since it was far too quiet and empty with his mother out of town.

Luckily, Carlos was there, lounging in the garden with his feet on the low stone wall of the terrace, staring moodily out at the blooming garden with a glass of rum in one hand.

He looked up when Adrian joined him, then gestured to the bottle on the table.

"I've already asked for a brandy," Adrian said, sitting down. "What did you discover?"

"There are two sorts of wagers," Carlos replied. His eyes unfocused as he cast back to his memories. Adrian was familiar with the look—Carlos had a mind like a steel box, holding every scrap of information tightly, and all he had to do was sort through it to recall the specific fact he needed. "The first is the slightly less offensive, and is a pool that simply offers bettors the option to choose a date by which Miss Blake is ruined."

"How are they to know that?"

Carlos held his response, because one of the footmen had come out with Adrian's brandy. After he withdrew to the house, Carlos continued.

"She either gets caught in a compromising position, or there is physical proof of the deed, like a bloodied sheet, though how the hell anyone could prove where a sheet came from without the lady to confirm it, I've got no idea," Carlos said a little doubtfully. "Or general condemnation of society following a big enough scandal that the Blakes cannot deny it, which is the outcome most are expecting. To be honest, after the initial flurry of wagers made the day after you were seen dancing with Miss Blake, very few men have placed a bet. I think most of them have steered clear of it, knowing that there's such murkiness about the actual event…not to mention that the whole notion is disgusting."

"You said there were two types of wager."

"Yes, the second has a much smaller number of bettors, thank God, but it's the one that's far more concerning. This is the wager that a man will be the one to ruin her. Essentially, each of these bettors is betting on himself to complete the deed by the date he set."

"Evans was one name."

"How'd you know?"

"He took Miss Blake for a ride in the park today and just happened to 'break' a wheel in a secluded area. Luckily I was passing and extracted her before any harm could be done."

"A broken wheel? Amateur," Carlos snorted. "But you're right. Evans stated he'd do it by Thursday. Evidently, Evans was drunk when he made the wager, and he's probably drunk now, because he'll probably lose now that you and Miss Blake are onto him. He wagered two hundred pounds, which he doesn't have."

"Who else?"

Carlos smiled meanly, saying, "I've written the names down for you. There's a half dozen that I could identify, and all of them deserve a dawn appointment." He handed Adrian a slip of paper.

"I'll reserve that option," Adrian said, taking a sip of the brandy as he read over the names. "But for now, I'd prefer to keep this whole situation as quiet as possible. Six duels in a week would create talk."

"And a new cemetery," Carlos added.

"Was Hynes mentioned? I thought he'd wager something, after being there that night."

"No, he wasn't. Perhaps he came to his senses?"

"Doubtful. He's not known for that. Several of these men are his cronies. Odd that he restrained himself."

"Gambling is expensive when you lose. He might simply be wary of a financial risk."

"No, he's quite wealthy." Adrian didn't like the omission, but he tried to focus on the names Carlos did bring him. He'd warn the Blakes that these men were not to be trusted around Rosalind.

"I could inform Mr. Blake. Or perhaps I could just tell Poppy," he mused out loud, not wanting to involve a barrister in the sordid news of an underworld wager. He'd probably want to bring the law into it.

"Hmm? What's that?"

"I was saying that it might be best to offer the names

to Miss St. George, who serves as Miss Blake's companion. She'll be best placed to guard her cousin from them."

"Let me do it," Carlos said. "That would be more discreet."

"That may be true. Tell her the names, but don't tell her the situation."

"Jesus, as if I'd explain such a wager to a young woman like her. You know, we might be making this unnecessarily complicated. Can't the family just go to the country?"

"Not soon enough. On our ride, Miss Blake mentioned that Mr. Blake is a barrister and has several important cases to argue. He can't leave the city until they are resolved."

"The ladies of the house could go ahead of him, though."

"Evidently, they do not have a second home themselves, and the rented house they normally stay at in the summers is not available until June."

"I suppose it would not do for you to offer the use of your country house," Carlos said, knowing full well it was out of the question.

"Can you see the gossips catching fire with that tidbit?" Adrian responded with a short laugh, seeing the humor in it, even though he was still irate about the whole thing. "No, we'll just find a way to get you and Miss St. George in the same spot for a few moments so you can give her those names. With luck, the whole business will stop there."

"Is she that formidable?"

"Oh, just wait." Adrian smiled as he thought of his friend going against Rose's cousin. At this point, he would not place a wager on who would survive the encounter.

Chapter 9

Dear Daisy,

Do you remember when you received the mysterious gift of a ballgown, and there was no name attached to the package? I am now in a position to fully appreciate how you felt. For the past several days, gifts have begun to arrive at the house every morning, and as they are unsigned, Mama has no satisfactory way to return them to the suspected sender. The first day it was chocolates, then freshly cut roses (don't worry, I couldn't accidentally be hurt by a thorn—they'd all been removed). Mama regarded them with horror and ordered Alice to throw them out on the dust heap. Luckily, Poppy intervened, pointing out that the roses would only last a few days, and it was a shame to not enjoy them, particularly as they could have been from anybody. What if we accidentally discarded a gift from the Prince Regent himself? How embarrassing would that be? (Not that it is likely, as I've never met him.)

On the next day, a boy delivered a box for me, again with no name attached. Alice asked who had ordered them, but the boy just shrugged and ran off. Well! The box proved to hold candied ginger, which you know I adore.

So does Mama, and she allowed me to keep the gift, after sampling a portion. What will arrive next? Who can say?

"Excuse me, misses, but you have visitors," Alice said from behind them.

Surprised by this announcement, Poppy turned in her seat, looking back at the maid. It was a few days after Rose's carriage debacle, and the girls had gone out to the garden in the back of the house to enjoy the spring warmth (as it was made clear neither of them should leave the property this day). Seated at the iron table near the house, Poppy decided it would be good to read and answer letters while they had the leisure. Rose had been dictating while Poppy wrote.

Poppy put down the pen and asked Alice, "Is it visiting hours already?" Had she lost track of time?

"No, miss. The gentlemen apologize, but say they would very much like to speak with you briefly. Both of you."

"More suitors for Rose?" Poppy asked wearily. "Give me their cards, and I'll decide if we even know them."

"It's Lord Norbury and a friend of his."

Rose, who'd been listening silently until now, looked suddenly interested. "Show them out here, Alice," she instructed before her cousin could object.

"Auntie would not like it," Poppy whispered.

"She's not here," Rose said. "And I'm curious why his lordship brought a companion. Perhaps he also needs a chaperone."

Poppy laughed at that, and capped the inkwell, then put a paperweight on the half-done letter.

Alice returned, followed by two men. Viscount Norbury was dressed as perfectly as ever, Poppy noted with the approval of one who knew. With a stepfather in the business of fabric imports, she'd seen very wealthy people try to purchase cut-rate fabrics, hoping to save money. The result was invariably sad, since not even the finest seamstress could work actual magic. Clothing made from poor fabric looked good at first, but didn't hold up to time and wear. However, Norbury didn't skimp on any part of his wardrobe. The wool of the pant legs was richly dyed, and the linen shirt snowy white under the brocade jacket.

Then her gaze drifted to the other man, and held there. She couldn't say what he was wearing, because she didn't notice. Norbury's companion was a little shorter than he, but possibly even more attractive. He had dark, alert eyes and a tiny smile on his lips. And he was looking directly at Poppy.

Norbury bowed, saying, "Good morning, ladies. We are scandalously early for calling, I know."

"Yet another way you flout convention, my lord," Poppy replied, wresting her attention from the other man…but not for long.

"Have I permission to introduce my friend to you both?" Adrian asked formally, which amused Poppy, considering that Adrian hadn't exactly followed protocol when they first met *him*.

Rose answered, "Certainly."

"Excellent. This is my very good friend, the inestimable Captain Carlos de la Guerra. Mr. de la Guerra, this is Miss Rosalind Blake and her cousin and companion, Miss Poppy St. George."

"Enchanted," de la Guerra said, bowing to each.

Poppy wasn't sure she was enchanted, but she decided to be polite for Rose's sake. Her cousin had already stood up and taken a step toward Norbury, and the viscount was quick to hold out his hands to guide her. Without even really announcing it, the two of them strolled in the direction of the heavily scented cut flower garden, leaving

Poppy with de la Guerra.

As they were already in the gardens, it seemed logical to accept the newcomer's offer of a turn around them. Poppy wasn't a fool—she recognized instantly that the sole purpose of bringing a companion along was to occupy Poppy's attention while Norbury got to speak to Rose alone. But since Poppy could see her cousin in the yard, albeit at a distance, she accepted the subterfuge.

So she walked along the gravel path with her new companion, wondering how he got roped into this escapade, thinking it would be rude to ask directly.

"How long have you known Lord Norbury?" she asked instead.

"Years," he said. "We met at Eton when we both started in the same form."

"Lord Norbury introduced you as Captain de la Guerra, and then as Mister."

"Yes. No title, I'm afraid."

She said, "I wasn't concerned about that. But shouldn't it be Señor de la Guerra?" She didn't know Spanish at all, but she was quite sure that the language didn't use "Mister."

"Usually, but when in Rome..." he replied with a shrug. "Or London, in this case."

"Are you from Spain?"

"No. I was born in Santo Domingo, on Hispaniola. That's in the Caribbean," he added.

"I know where it is," Poppy returned tartly. "I can read a map."

"So you're a lady of some learning," he said with what sounded like heavy sarcasm to her ears.

Oh, this was not going well, Poppy thought. She set her jaw and reminded herself that Rose would appreciate a few more minutes with Norbury.

De la Guerra asked what she and Rose did to amuse themselves, and Poppy mentioned that they had a number of pursuits, from music to museums, not to mention the occasional excursion, such a planned visit to Vauxhall Gardens the next evening.

"Never been," he said to that.

So much for a polite discussion of Vauxhall's charms. She tried again. "He called you Captain. Why?"

"Because I have a ship, of which I am captain." The shortness of the answer made Poppy think that she wasn't the only person annoyed by this conversation.

"Here in London? What's its name?"

"Her name is *Agustina*," he said, suddenly warming up to the subject. "Ships are female, you know. Which only makes sense. They're temperamental, demanding, and can lead a man to his doom. But treated well, they can offer the whole world. A fair exchange."

"Why Agustina?" Poppy asked, ignoring a tiny thrill in her stomach when he spoke. It was probably just more irritation. He seemed like a very irritating man. "Is it a family name?"

"No, I chose it to honor Agustina of Aragón, a brave patriot who defended the city walls in battle."

"Oh, I like *that*." Poppy envisioned a woman dumping pitch on armies below, her hair gleaming in the sun.

"I thought you might, Miss St. George."

"Did you? You just met me. How could you guess anything about what I might like or dislike?"

He shot her a sidelong glance, then said, with no trace of humor, "I hope you like protecting those who need it."

Chapter 10

"WHERE IS POPPY?" ROSE ASKED Lord Norbury as they stepped past a cloud of lilac aroma on the way out of the cut flower garden.

"She's near those tall trees on the north side of the yard, walking with Mr. de la Guerra. They do not appear to be at odds, and no one has drawn a weapon yet."

"Well, that's something," Rose said. "Poppy does tend to scare off gentlemen."

"She may find him more difficult to intimidate than most. Here's that bench under the chestnut tree. Have a seat, Miss Blake."

So they sat in the back garden of the house, under the dappled, light shade of a tree just leafing out, and Rose could feel the sun's warmth seeping through the branches. She knew the servants were no doubt keeping a very close watch on the garden from a window of the house, but she didn't mind, because it was a small victory just be able to spend a little time without a chaperone hovering.

Then again, Lord Norbury was being extremely careful, even bringing along another person to help populate the area. Aloud she said, "People call you a rake, but it's not quite accurate, is it?"

"You wound me, Miss Blake. Next you'll be saying I'm a pillar of society."

"Never that," Rose promised. "I just meant that your reputation is, well, a little simplified."

"Go on. This conversation is taking a fascinating turn."

"You've had…affairs," she said, the very term feeling transgressive to speak out loud.

"Dozens," he admitted, sounding quite complacent about it.

"But an affair…well, it's a matter between you and the lady."

"You'd be surprised at how often the husband has an opinion," he corrected.

Rose laughed, knowing she shouldn't. "That aside, I mean that the lady *wants* to have an affair. She's quite willing, even…eager?"

"If you mean that the ladies are often the ones to seek me out and initiate the affair, you are correct."

"How do they do that? I mean, there's not some secret signal, is there?" Rose was so curious about this forbidden realm of society. "How do they know to approach *you*?"

"Hmm, that last question is easier. My reputation is self-perpetuating, in the sense that since I am known to be an ardent and attentive lover—I'm not being boastful, merely repeating the consensus—so the bored wives and widows of London set their sights on me and all I have to do is pick."

"Then it's mutual. You're not harming a woman's marriage prospects or her family's reputation."

"Not if I can help it." He inhaled, a breath deep enough for Rose to hear the tension in him, then he said, "I have to admit that I've made mistakes. Some of my earlier exploits were dicey. As a younger man, I had not quite understood the rules—young men are allowed to blunder and I blundered quite a bit. I picked my lovers based on their attractiveness and my mood, which led to a few misunderstandings."

"So there are rules?"

"Oh, yes. Affairs may be safely conducted with widows, or wives who've already borne heirs, thus securing the family line. Such women are relatively free to discreetly pursue their own interests."

"And have you a mistress? Most gentlemen do, is that true?"

"Some do. It's perfectly accepted to have a lover of a lower class, or a kept mistress, but many men don't. I don't."

"Why not?"

He paused, for so long that Rose decided her questions were quite beyond the pale and even he was offended by them. Then he said, "It's too like indentured servitude. A mistress is kept, you know. She's offered financial protection and other such benefits. I don't like the idea that I can't be sure if a woman was interested in me, or merely in the comfortable life I could provide."

"But surely you can't be so concerned," Rose teased. "After all, your reputation…"

He took her hand. "No, everyone is concerned with what others think of them, even those who pretend they don't care one whit."

"Like you."

"Like me. You're full of interesting questions, Miss Blake. What has brought all this on?"

She thought about it for a moment, then confessed, "No one tells us *anything*. Ladies, that is. Poppy and I have so many questions about so many things, but everyone wants to keep us wrapped in cotton, as if we're china that will shatter with the least nudge."

"To be fair, they are trying to protect you."

"Ah, yes, because if we eat from the tree of knowledge, we'll all become little Eves, sinning for the rest of our days," Rose said, rather bitterly.

"They have your best interests at heart," Adrian reminded her. "As I said, young men are allowed to blunder. Young women are not."

"It's not fair."

"No," he agreed. "But that's the world we live in."

About to expound on the injustice of it all, Rose suddenly paused, hearing something strange in the corners of her perception. A sort of desperate sound, but very faint.

She put her hand on Adrian's arm, signaling him to keep silent. "Did you hear that?" she whispered. "There's something...distressed...I think...over there." She pointed in the direction the sound was coming from. "Maybe near the rosebushes?"

"Stay," Adrian told her. "I'll go and find out what it is."

He left her and walked in the same direction. The sound stopped for a moment, and then resumed, louder.

"What the..." Adrian muttered, and then Rose heard the sound of rustling leaves as Adrian dove into the rosebush.

* * * *

On the other side of the garden, Poppy walked with Mr. de la Guerra, covertly assessing him while she also tried to keep an eye on Rose and Lord Norbury. The last time she looked, they were sitting on a broad stone bench in full view of nearly the whole yard, so Poppy could devote only a small part of her attention to them, and the rest to the new gentleman, and his startling pronounce-ment.

"Of course I like protecting those who need it. What sort of person doesn't?"

"This is going to sound very odd, Miss St. George, and while you have no reason to trust me, I hope that you will."

"That is not an auspicious beginning, Mr. de la Guer-ra."

"Norbury asked me to come here for a specific pur-pose. This is not purely a social call. I am going to give you a list of names. They are the names of people who should not be admitted to this house, or ever allowed to be near Miss Blake."

"Excuse me?" She hadn't been expecting *that*.

He handed her a folded note, and Poppy took it and opened it.

"Mr. Evans has already been disinvited," she said, reading the first name.

"Good."

Poppy continued on, frowning. "These next three gen-tlemen all called at the house the same day. The day af-ter…" She looked up at him. "What is this? What hap-pened that night, besides Lord Norbury rescuing Rose from Mr. Hynes's prank?"

"The details are not important."

"I beg to differ, Mr. de la Guerra. You ask me to trust you, but you provide no basis for it."

"That's the meaning of trust."

"No, that's the meaning of naiveté," she countered, annoyed by his attitude. Did he really think she was just going to do whatever he said? "Rose relies on me, and I won't be led around by the nose just for the amusement of some men who enjoy toying with a girl's life."

"Norbury isn't toying."

"You're his friend. You'd say that no matter what."

"I *am* his friend, but it's still true." De la Guerra looked sincere, for what that was worth. "He feels that he got Miss Blake some unwanted notoriety, so he's just trying to see her through it without further damage."

"Wouldn't the best way to do that be to simply avoid her? *I* can protect Rose from unwanted suitors."

"I'm sure you can...unless someone starts breaking the rules. Like Mr. Evans did."

"Wait, you know what happened?" Poppy asked, appalled.

"Adrian—Norbury, that is—told me. I assure you it won't go further. Not that I live in the circles who would care about such news," he added.

"Even so, a stray comment could—what in the world is he *doing*?" Poppy suddenly asked. Instinctively, she grabbed de la Guerra by the arm and pointed to where Lord Norbury was just diving into a thorn bush.

De la Guerra raised an eyebrow. "Hmm, that's unconventional, even for Adrian. Let's go find out."

* * * *

Rose was waiting anxiously for Adrian to report what he found, and when Poppy and Mr. de la Guerra rushed up, demanding answers (well, Poppy demanded answers), Rose didn't have many to give.

"I heard something strange and Lord Norbury went to investigate. I didn't expect him to investigate quite so..."

"Actively?" Poppy suggested. "He's going to ruin his jacket. I always told Auntie Gertrude to have that shrubbery removed because the thorns are a menace."

"Norbury, do we have to send someone in after you?"

de la Guerra called, sounding not terribly concerned.

"Everyone hush," Adrian called back, his voice muffled. "I'm busy."

"Doing what?" his friend asked.

"*Hush*," Rose told him, echoed by both Poppy and Adrian.

There was a moment of extremely awkward silence, broken only by the rustling of leaves.

Then Rose heard a high-pitched squeak, and Norbury pronounced in triumph, "Ha! Got you!"

"What is happening?" Rose asked.

Norbury made his way back to the safety of the lawn.

"Oh, sir! Your jacket is *destroyed*," Poppy declared in chagrin.

"I have more," he said carelessly, even as he moved toward Rose. "Hold out your arms," he told her.

"Why?" she asked.

"Because you have rescued a kitten," Adrian declared. He carefully placed a small ball of fluff into Rose's waiting arms. For a moment, she felt his hands against her arms, warm and gentle as he stroked the little mewling creature.

"It's all right," he crooned, "We've got you. Rose will take care of you now. You're not much more than mud and fur, are you? You need a good meal and a bath before you'll be allowed among society."

She marveled at how gently he spoke to the cat, how utterly different his tone was to the sharp, bored voice he used when around most people.

"What color is it?" Rose asked. She cradled the cat next to her body, loving the animal's warmth and the kitten's tiny meow of inquiry.

"Muddy, to be honest. But I suspect it will be revealed as a good, honest tabby cat."

"Auntie won't like this," Poppy murmured.

"I've always wanted a cat!" Rose said, delighted. "Thank you, my lord!"

"You're the one who heard it mewling. Is it *still* mewling?"

"No, it's purring...." Rose hesitated, because she did hear a meowing sound. But it wasn't coming from the kitten in her arms. She tipped her head, turning her ear to better catch the source of the noise. Frowning, she looked up. "It's coming from above somehow. Poppy?" she asked, prompting her cousin to confirm what she heard.

Poppy said, "I hear it too. There must be another kitten stuck somewhere. Oh, Auntie will *hate* this."

* * * *

Poppy listened harder, and pointed to a tree that branched above the rosebush. "I think the other kitten must have climbed up there and got stuck. It's going to starve up there, or fall out. We can't reach it all the way up there."

"I'll get it," de la Guerra said.

"You can't do that!"

"Watch me. And don't worry, only one jacket needs to die this day," he replied, already divesting himself of his jacket. He handed it to Poppy as if that were a normal thing to do. Mouth slightly agape, she took the jacket and folded it over her arm, trying very hard not to notice the lingering body heat in the fabric.

De la Guerra plunged into the greenery surrounding the tree in question, leaving the others to wait.

"Not how I expected to spend the morning," Norbury commented with his usual complacent air.

"I do hope your friend won't do something risky,"

Rose added, holding the first kitten to her chest.

"That would be a false hope, Miss Blake."

And indeed, de la Guerra had already begun to climb the trunk of the tree, moving easily as he got higher and higher, finally reaching the main branch the kitten's cries seemed to be coming from.

"He's going to break his neck," Poppy muttered.

"He's climbed masts in storms, Miss St. George. I doubt this excursion will be the one to finish him off."

Nevertheless, Poppy worried. She watched as the man clambered out onto the branch. He acted very confident, and she had to admit he seemed to know what he was doing. Then the sleeve of his shirt caught on a stray branch and he cursed in Spanish as he lurched to the side, almost losing his balance.

"Oh, Lord," Poppy breathed, sure he was about to crash to the ground.

De la Guerra steadied himself, then actually pulled the shirt off his body, tying it around his waist to keep it from catching on another branch.

The leaves hid some his body, but there was still far more male figure visible than Poppy had ever seen in her whole life.

Norbury made a sound like a stifled laugh. Poppy tried to look away, but then gave up, sure that the moment she did so, de la Guerra would fall.

He got to the thinner section of the branch, which bent alarmingly. He reached forward, moving with agonizing slowness. He extracted something small from a clump of leaves, and then backed up to the wider part of the main branch.

Poppy took a cautious breath, hoping the worst was over. And then nearly shrieked, because de la Guerra suddenly swung to the bottom of the branch, with only one hand holding on. He dropped to the ground, disappearing into the thicker shrubbery.

"Are you dead?" Norbury called.

"Not yet," de la Guerra answered, sounding cheerful and very much alive.

Poppy exhaled, then inhaled once more as de la Guerra emerged from the living wall of the plants, shirtless and smiling. He held a small gray creature in his hand, and he walked directly up to Poppy.

"This one must be yours, Miss St. George," he said, handing it to her.

Poppy took it, still staring at his bare skin, which was deeply tanned and quite smooth, except for several slightly raised tattoos on his well-muscled arms and chest.

Norbury cleared his throat meaningfully, and de la Guerra stepped away, untying the rolled-up shirt and putting it on again. He accepted his jacket from Poppy's outstretched arm, and within a moment, he looked vaguely respectable again.

Her cheeks burning, Poppy devoted her attention to the kitten while he dressed. The tiny gray cat had china-blue eyes, and white-tipped ears. It mewed at Poppy in inquiry, and she said, "It's all right now, little one. We'll take care of you until we find your mother...if you still have a mother." Judging by how scrawny the kitten felt, she rather doubted it. Had the kittens been abandoned?

Just then, a voice boomed out from near the house. "Whatever is going on here?" It was Mr. Blake, looking rather upset.

Rose turned to the house, calling back, "Our guests have just rescued two kittens! Isn't it wonderful?"

It was difficult for anyone to tell Rose a thing *wasn't* wonderful when she was so happy and smiling like she was in that moment. Poppy just hoped that the presence of the kittens might divert the attention of Mr. Blake from the fact that one of the men in the garden was a total stranger to him.

"We'd better get this sorted immediately," Poppy told the others in a low voice. They all moved to the terrace. Poppy saw the table and the half-written letter there, feeling that part of the morning happened a lifetime ago.

Mr. Blake handled the introduction of Mr. de la Guerra well enough, accepting that he was a friend of Lord Norbury without thinking much more about it (thankfully, the man *had* got his jacket back on very quickly).

Mr. Blake was frowning in puzzlement at the kittens. "Where did these come from?"

"They were in the garden, and Lord Norbury and Mr. de la Guerra retrieved them. I believe they're extremely hungry."

"Well, Cook will have something for them," Mr. Blake said. "Why don't you girls go to the kitchen and find out. The gentlemen must have other calls to make."

"Indeed, sir," Norbury said easily, obviously catching the implicit command. "We are glad to have been of service, unexpected as the form of it was."

De la Guerra echoed this, and even bowed over Poppy's free hand (the other being occupied holding a squirming kitten).

"Come, come," Mr. Blake said. "Let's get these kittens tended to. Haven't you got to prepare for your performance tonight, Rose?"

"Performance?" de la Guerra echoed, confused.

"Rose is going to perform at Lady Selby's tonight, as part of a little musicale evening. I think there will be one professional signer invited, but the others are all just enthusiasts." Poppy felt the need to explain, for typically young ladies like Rose would never perform in public.

"Then we will not distract you further," Norbury said. "Good day, ladies."

Poppy held the kitten closer when it tried to leap out of her arms toward de la Guerra. "Oh, no," she murmured. "You're staying right here."

De la Guerra glanced back at her just once, and Poppy didn't dare return his smile, for fear he'd take it as interest. She was not at all interested in him. The memory of him half-naked flashed in front of her mind again.

No, not interested at all.

Chapter 11

AFTER THE MEN LEFT THE Blake house, Carlos assured Adrian that he gave the list of names of Miss St. George, and that he hadn't revealed any of the reason why, though he added, "Good thing the cats appeared, because she was going to demand an explanation. They were an excellent distraction."

"Not to mention that fact that you half disrobed in front of the women."

"Well, your Rose couldn't see me and be scandalized, so what do you care?" Carlos replied with a shrug. "I assume that you'll be finding a way to attend that music... thing...tonight."

"Want me to secure an invitation for you as well? Miss St. George is certain to be there."

"Oh, no, I'm quite done entertaining debutantes. I'm happy to help you, but I don't want to be mistaken for a lovesick suitor. Anyway, I've got some actual business to attend to."

Carlos bid him goodbye and hailed a carriage to take him into the city, where he would conduct whatever business his family required of him.

Meanwhile, Adrian headed for his club. Once there, he dashed off a short message to Lady Selby, mentioning that

he heard of some musician in town, had she heard anything of it? One of club's servants took it to be sent via a
messenger. Adrian expected a reply within the hour. Lady
Selby would pounce on the chance to invite the viscount
to her event, if only to show off her acumen at choosing
entertainment.

He was wrong.

It took an hour *and* ten minutes to receive Lady Selby's reply. Adrian smiled when he read her note insisting
that he was more than welcome to attend her home
tonight, where the musicians would be offering an exclusive performance following supper.

Adrian had no intention of suffering through a formal
dinner, but he'd arrive in time for the music, mostly to
hear Rose play the pianoforte. She'd sounded so enthused
about her practice, and he was curious to hear the result of
all that dedication.

* * * *

The musicale was a bigger event than Poppy had
thought it would be. She and Rose were both dressed in
their finest spring gowns, Rosalind in antique lace and
Poppy in white lawn. But Poppy whispered to Rose about
the extravagance of some other guests, who looked like a
scene from the *Arabian Nights*. "I could have emptied my
jewelry box and still not be noticed among this crowd,"
Poppy said, feeling very much like a tradesman's daughter all of a sudden.

"Oh, something tells me we'll be noticed now," Rose
whispered back.

Rosalind's words came true almost instantly, as her
instructor, Maestro Valdi, sighted them and made his way
over. He was filled with delight at seeing his student, and

in his broken English, heavily peppered with excited Italian, he made it clear that the performance tonight was not to be missed.

"Lady Selby, she has an ear, you know," he said. "She brings the finest, the top rank to London. You will hear tonight—these musicians, they will make you weep with joy."

Rosalind listened avidly to Valdi's gossip regarding the performers. Poppy only nodded politely, since she was scanning the crowd for familiar faces. She almost jumped when she saw one she did not expect. Jonathan Hynes, dressed in his usual black velvet coat and cavalierly tied cravat, was staring in her direction, his face a mask.

Poppy, remembering the man's prank on Rosalind, unconsciously drew in her breath. What was he doing here, and why was he focused on her and Rosalind? Before Poppy could turn away, his lips curled up in a cruel smile. She deliberately cast her gaze elsewhere, pretending she hadn't noticed him. But she didn't like it. Not at all.

Soon enough, the guests were seated in the music room, and the performance began. Rosalind was entranced by the first few pieces, sung by an Italian soprano with a voice like silver. Poppy fidgeted, her mind on other things.

Then she glanced backward and to her surprise, she saw none other than Viscount Norbury in the back row, his eyes locked on Rose.

* * * *

Adrian sat back in the chair, glad he was toward the rear of the room. In general, he hated these sorts of occasions. He could feel the eyes of the other guests on him, as if he were a tiger about to pounce on the nearest available female. They never understood he was a tiger with taste—none of the people present here held any interest for him.

Except Rosalind. She was fascinating. Her blindness gave her a very different understanding of life, and while she played the part of young lady of the gentry perfectly, for that was how she was brought up, it was clear that her mind was working the whole time, drawing different inferences and conclusions, alert to nuances in people's words and tone that other people missed entirely. Talking with Rose was always surprising, and Adrian had not been surprised in a long, long time.

After the invited musician bowed and left the front of the room, Rose stood up, and Poppy led her to the center of the cleared area in front of the pianoforte, this house being laid out much differently than her own home.

Adrian straightened up, curious. Why was Rose not sitting at the piano? He understood that instrument to be her focus.

Instead it was Poppy who walked to the piano and struck a single key, sounding a clear tone into the otherwise silent air. Rose nodded, then inhaled, her chest and belly swelling subtly.

She opened her mouth and began to sing unaccompanied. It was just her voice flowing into the room, filling the void with pure bel canto sound.

The words were Italian, and Adrian didn't understand a single one of them, and he didn't need to, because he felt as if Rose were singing directly to him, spilling out her soul in spun-glass notes.

The music wrapped itself around him, warm and sensuous, like velvet in the air. When she held a particular note, a long *ah* of an aching heart, Adrian felt it reverberate in his ears and lungs, winding its way into his body until he felt it everywhere, inescapable in its longing.

How was it possible that Rose had such incredible talent and no one ever mentioned it, not once? Adrian wanted nothing more than to hear her sing all night. He'd listen gratefully, and anyone who got restless could damn well leave. In fact, he wanted everyone else to leave so that Rose sung for him and him alone.

The performance ended far too soon. Everyone applauded, except for Adrian, who sat there stunned, still recovering from the rapture of the song.

When he managed to pull himself together, he approached the front of the room where Rose stood with Poppy. (The elder Blakes were chatting with other guests at the side of the room.) He said, almost accusingly, "You never told me that you sing."

"I suppose you only heard me practicing at the piano," Rose replied, as if she'd not just upended his world. "I've been studying both pianoforte and voice with Maestro Valdi for years. He said that if I'd been born in different circumstances, I could have run away and joined an opera company."

"He never said that in Mrs. Blake's presence," Poppy added dryly. "She'd have apoplexy at the thought of her daughter on a stage."

Adrian nodded, for it was true. Regardless of talent, young women of Rose's social class would have to give up everything to perform professionally. Such a decision would be seen as the equivalent of becoming a prostitute—and to be fair, considering that a significant number of actresses and singers also supported themselves by offering certain favors to patrons, this assumption was often correct.

So Rose would only ever perform in places like this,

parties of indulgent gentry and small family gatherings, where such entertainments were only for diversion, and nothing more than praise would ever be offered.

"You have a rare skill," Adrian said, wishing he could say what he really felt, which was that Rose's voice ripped several layers of armor off his soul, layers he put in place very carefully, over years...and he didn't even mind.

"I'm glad you enjoyed the music," Rose said with a pleased smile on her face.

Enjoyed wasn't a strong enough word, but he smiled back all the same.

He bowed and turned to leave, not wanting to bring too much attention to him being near Rose. He walked toward the doors, before he got ensnared in some dire conversation with the other guests. Just as he reached the doorway, Mr. Blake said, "Halt there, my lord."

Adrian looked back and raised an eyebrow. He was in general not used to being told to *halt*, as if he were a mule on the way to market. "What is it, sir?"

The older man was graying and portly, but he had an unmistakable energy. "I wish to have a word."

"Then have it."

Blake glanced around the busy room. "Come with me, for what I have to say is a sensitive matter."

He led Adrian down the hallway to the library. A fire burned low in the hearth, and candles burned in sconces along the walls, brightening the space.

He sat down in the chair opposite Dillon Blake, sensing that he was about to hear something he didn't want to. He proved to be correct in his assessment.

"I think it would be best if you did not call at my house again," Mr. Blake said, opening with the blunt statement as if he were arguing before the bar and needed to state his case quickly.

"Have I offended you in some way, sir? I assure you the kittens were not a planned addition to the family."

"Never mind the kittens!" Blake said. "I am concerned about Rose. Let us not pretend that you are of spotless reputation, my lord. The longer you are seen calling on her, the more dangerous it is for our girl."

Adrian knew where this was going, and he needed to head it off. "I disagree, sir. In fact, the longer I am seen calling at your house, the safer Miss Blake's reputation is."

"How's that?"

"Well, just think of the appearance, sir. Calling at the house as I have, during regular social hours and among the whole household and other guests…that is very dull. Clearly I cannot be doing this without your knowledge and approval, and your knowledge and approval means that nothing untoward could possibly be going on. What is less prone to gossip than what is out in the open, fully sanctioned and utterly without intrigue?"

Blake frowned, thinking his way through that argument.

Adrian went on. "Yes, it's likely that some folks in London think I've lost my head for enjoying the company of young ladies such as Miss Blake and Miss St. George. I am expected to only desire dissolute, dangerous entertainment. But that is nonsense, and it says more about those people talking than it does about me. Indeed, all it really tells us is that London society has missed two ladies of great charm. Though Miss Poppy *might* hold her tongue a bit to spare the unwary," he added.

"That girl!" Blake sighed, momentarily distracted. "She does speak her mind." He shook his head in despair.

Adrian leaned forward. "Sir, if I were to abruptly

cease calling at your house, the gossips would notice *that*, and assume that there is a reason, and they will dream up the wildest reasons they can. Let me continue to visit, and everyone will be bored by the lack of news."

"Possibly," Mr. Blake murmured.

"Summer is practically upon us. I escape to my country estate for those months, and when I return to London for next Season, this will all be forgotten." In truth, Adrian didn't fancy the idea of leaving town just yet, or of implying that he'd not see Rose in the future. But if that's what it took to calm Mr. Blake's concerns, it would do. And with the echo of Rose's song still in his ears, Adrian found himself wanting any excuse to see her again.

"I suppose that makes sense," Mr. Blake said, mulling it over. "And who knows, by the end of summer, Rose might have a proposal in hand, and then all will be well. The best solution, really. It is nice that several potential suitors call at the house now. Took them long enough, but perhaps that incident at the ball was what it took to get her noticed. Have you got an opinion on any of these gentlemen?"

"I don't know any of them well enough to say," Adrian replied cautiously, not hinting that he tended to loathe any other man who tried to get Rose's attention. Especially cads like Mr. Evans, who had a vested interest in making Rose's life a wreck. "Have any of them asked for permission to"—he could barely get the word out—"marry her?"

"Not yet. Too early, I expect. But it is encouraging. *If* Poppy doesn't frighten them off."

"Indeed, sir." Privately, Adrian hoped Poppy sent every single one of them running for the hills.

"Then you may continue to associate with my daughter, so long as *she* does not object."

"Miss Blake is no child. She is intelligent and quite capable of deciding who to spend her time with. If she chooses not to receive me, I should of course leave her be." Adrian leaned closer, his voice hot. "But I will let no one insinuate that my actions are less than honorable. Do I make myself clear?"

"Perfectly," Blake said, just as hot. "Though it's a bit late in the game for you to trumpet your *honor*." He left before Adrian could form a suitable reply.

He sat back in the chair, thinking hard.

Why the hell had he argued so fiercely for the mere right to see Rose? He and Carlos had given the list of dangerous names to Poppy. The family had the responsibility to protect their own daughter. Adrian could walk away this instant.

But he didn't want to. He closed his eyes and heard Rose's voice in his head again. He couldn't walk away from that. And he couldn't let anyone destroy such beauty.

Chapter 12

DEAR CAMELLIA,

Much has happened since we wrote to you last. The most important change is the increased size of the Blake household. Two new kittens have joined us, one for Poppy, one for me! They were rescued from the wilds of the back garden, by two gentleman callers who proved up to the challenge. I am told that mine is a tabby, and Poppy's a darling little gray furball. When you have the time, you must visit and meet them. (The cats, not the men! —Poppy)

Please know that we are thinking of your mother now, and hope that she is on the mend...

Rose and Poppy had stayed at Lady Selby's house very late last evening, and they got back home in the small hours. Poppy had announced that she could see the eastern sky growing pale by the time the girls finally climbed into their beds. Unsurprisingly, they slept till nearly noon.

Rose woke first, lolling in bed, enjoying the soft touch of a spring breeze through the open window. She listened to the chirping of dozens of birds in the yard outside, and cuddled into her bedding, the cotton pillowcase smooth and cool against her cheek. Then she brushed her hand against fur, and heard a mewing.

"Oh, I've got a cat," she murmured.

"Me too," Poppy said from her bed. "They seem to like sleeping in beds better than on the ground."

"Quite reasonable." Rose petted the small kitten, who began to purr loudly. "To think that yesterday morning we didn't have these darling little creatures!"

"The men did show great zeal in rescuing them," Poppy agreed with a dry tone that Rose couldn't quite understand.

"Wasn't that a noble act?"

"Hmmmm" was all Poppy said. "Perhaps not entirely."

"I hope you were not too bored by Lord Norbury's friend."

"How could I be bored when the day included the rescue of wild animals and Mr. de la Guerra scaling an oak tree as easily as I climb a staircase?"

"Lord Norbury suggested you two were getting along while you were walking the garden path...before the cat rescue."

"I wouldn't say that," Poppy sniffed. "He's extremely high-handed and thinks he's always correct and he thinks he's smarter than everyone else."

"Oh, so just like you, then," Rose noted blandly.

"Not like me at all! I don't associate with notorious rogues, and make fun of British society—"

Rose chuckled. "You do make fun of British society, on an almost daily basis."

"Well, I don't sail the sea, crisscrossing the Caribbean on whatever adventures he chooses to have."

"It sounds exciting."

"What shall you name your cat? Did you have any ideas after sleeping?" Poppy asked, clearly trying to change the subject. "I think it's a him."

Just then, the kitten stretched and flexed out thin, needle-sharp claws. It raked Rose's forearm as it did so, making her wince. "Ooooh, stop that," she told the cat, pulling the offending paw away to a safer distance. "You're a regular rakehell, aren't you?"

Poppy laughed. "So he is. Rakehell! But we'll need a different name to use in polite company. Your mother would kick him out the door if she realized we called him such."

After a few moments of intense discussion, it was decided that the cat's formal name would be Sir Ralph, to be secretly known as Ralph the Rakehell when Rose's mother was not in earshot.

"And yours?" Rose asked. "It's a girl cat, correct?"

"I believe so. She's a silvery gray, like the fog. I think I shall call her Miss Mist."

"Oh, she already sounds adorable. I wonder if she would object to a bow around her neck."

"Ha, I've got some satin ribbon remnants at the warehouse. I'll try them out. I could sew Ralph a little cravat if you like."

Before Rose could answer that ridiculous proposal, Alice entered and routed them out of bed with the news that a bouquet of flowers waited downstairs for Rose, and that they had a letter from their schoolfriend Miss Swift.

"Oh, we should read it before we finish the letter we're writing to her! I wonder what Lia is up to this summer. Wouldn't it be nice to see her while she's still in town?"

Rose agreed, and allowed Alice to dress her in a lightweight summer gown of soft cotton. Ralph the Rakehell mewed from his spot on Rose's pillow, and Rose said, "Oh, you must be hungry. So am I!"

"I told Cook to hold the breakfast things. Your parents got up rather late too, miss," Alice informed them.

Ralph jumped down from the bed and joined the procession to the dining room. Miss Mist (who'd scouted ahead) was already there, lapping a saucer of cream set down next to Mr. Blake's seat.

The arrival of two small cats in the house had brought mixed reactions. Alice declared them to be the sweetest creatures in London, while her mother hinted darkly that any damage to the draperies would result in exile for the kittens. Mr. Blake seemed to have sided with Alice, judging by the dish of cream.

"Ralph can have the rest of the cream," Rose declared when she heard what was going on. "We don't want him to starve."

"Not a chance of that, the way the little beast devours things," her mother said. And if they bring us any dead mice…" she said, trailing off. Rose did not need eyes to know that her mother was shuddering.

"You hate mice," Rose pointed out. "You should want a creature that will keep them away from the house. Cook will like our new pets very much, I'm sure. She's always complaining of pests in the kitchen." Indeed, Cook fought a protracted war with the rodents of the world, deploying rat poison liberally.

Alice then entered, accompanied by the heady scent of flowers wafting through the air.

"This bouquet was sent this morning for Miss Rose," Alice announced, placing the vase on the table with a muffled thud, suggesting a heavy burden.

"Lilies," she said, inhaling. "How beautiful."

Unsurprisingly, the anonymous gift became the topic of conversation. It was unavoidable, since the hothouse flowers permeated the foyer and drifted into the dining room, their scent rich and somehow suggestive. The lilies in the garden never smelled quite like this.

"More gifts," her mother tutted. "With no note, again."

A note should not be necessary, Rosalind thought. The flowers spoke for themselves. She smiled, inhaling again. "I like them. Alice, have them taken up to my room, please."

"Rosalind!" her mother gasped. "You can't have—"

"Flowers in my room?" Rosalind asked. "Will the flowers seduce me, Mother?"

"I don't think you understand—"

"I don't. Flowers are meant to be enjoyed. I want the lilies in my room." Rosalind sensed her mother relenting, and reveled in this one small victory.

"I'm glad we're going to Vauxhall this evening," Poppy said suddenly. "It will be good to get some fresh air. Rose is looking a little pale, isn't she, Aunt?"

"I feel fine…" Rosalind began.

"No, I think you need fresh air," her cousin insisted.

"We will all go," her mother said.

"Perhaps there will be fireworks," Mr. Blake said brightly. He was a man of simple pleasures, and a fireworks display delighted him as much as winning a case.

* * * *

Vauxhall Gardens was a popular destination for the *ton*, especially in spring, when the flowers bloomed everywhere and the newly leafed trees provided a glorious canopy overhead. The gardens were lovely by day, but evening made them enchanting, with lanterns glowing to illuminate the park. It also helped that not all the paths were so well-lit. Many a couple had found a spot in Vauxhall where a few kisses, or more, could be shared out of the view of others.

For her part, Rosalind was glad just to get out of the house. This night, she wore a simply cut dress of dark green silk, pale yellow gloves, and a lace shawl. Poppy always selected the colors she wore, but Rosalind chose the fabrics themselves, so she could revel in the textures and weights of them all. This particular gown fit closely around the bust, and then fell loosely below the empire waist. It felt pretty, and her cousin assured her it also looked so.

Mr. Blake ordered a large coach to accommodate the four of them. They alighted at the entrance to Vauxhall, Rose overhearing the rustle and murmur of many people. On such a warm spring night, it was no surprise the gardens were packed.

The whole family took a turn around the main lawn. Then Mrs. Blake declared she wanted refreshments, heading toward a spot where tables had been set out to serve those enjoying the gardens. A quartet played charming music in one corner, and couples danced not far away. They all sat for a time, sipping tart lemonade from tall glasses, and chatting about the day's events. But Rosalind, hearing the plaintive violin and the dozens of conversations around her, grew restless.

"I should like to walk a bit more, Mama," she said. "I sat all day."

Poppy moved. "I want a stroll too. It's such a beautiful night. Do you mind, Aunt Gertrude? You both can stay here and rest. We won't be long."

"Be careful, dears," Rose's mother warned, as if there were thieves in the shrubbery.

The girls quickly took their leave, arms entwined.

"I thought I'd go mad if I kept having to sit there," Poppy confessed. "I'm rather antsy."

"Yes, though I'm just happy to be outside," Rosalind said. They proceeded down a side path fragrant with early flowers. The sounds of the crowd faded behind them. "This is lovely," Rosalind sighed, relishing the peace of the night. She stifled the slight feeling of loneliness that had been dogging her the past few days. Though she should not have gotten used to Adrian's presence after only a few days, she missed him.

Just then, she sensed someone approaching.

A warm voice said, "Good evening, ladies."

"Lord Norbury," Poppy replied first, her tone polite but still skeptical. "What a coincidence to see you here. And is that Mr. de la Guerra haunting the path alongside you?"

"Enchanted, as ever," a second voice said rather sarcastically. Rose hadn't even heard him approach, he was so quiet.

"I wonder if I could persuade your ever-vigilant chaperone to wander off for just a moment," Adrian said to Rose, and she let him take her hands in his own. "Not too far, of course. And she'll be escorted by Mr. de la Guerra."

"As if that reassures me," Poppy said.

Rose bit her lip. "Please, Poppy? Just for a few moments?"

Her cousin's indecision was agonizing. But then Poppy took a breath and said, "Very well. Five minutes and not a moment longer."

"Thank you!" Rose smiled in her direction.

"Scream if he even thinks of doing something improper," Poppy warned. She muttered something to de la Guerra and then Rose heard them walking farther down the path.

Then they were alone.

Chapter 13

POPPY ALLOWED MR. DE LA Guerra to take her arm, despite her extreme doubts about the whole situation.

Carlos de la Guerra seemed to be determined to hover around her. Poppy was annoyed (or rather, she tried to maintain a sense of annoyance). But he was a difficult person to simply dismiss. Whenever she was about to tell him his attentions were onerous, he managed to crack a wry joke or make an observation about the crowd that had Poppy biting her lip to keep from laughing out loud.

"This whole thing is your fault," Poppy accused him.

"What do you mean?"

"You know exactly what I mean! While you were at the house before your infamous cat rescue, I just happened to mention that the family intended to go to Vauxhall Gardens tonight, and then you told Lord Norbury we'd likely be here and he was able to get a moment alone with Rose."

Carlos pointed out, "You didn't have to leave her."

"But Rose so wanted to talk with him alone. And she's hard to say no to."

"I think it was sweet of you," Carlos said. "Anyway, Norbury is careful about not getting caught for such things—doubly so now."

"Why doubly so now?" Poppy asked, puzzled.

Carlos looked briefly chagrined, but then said, "I just meant that because Miss Blake is...unable to be as aware as other young ladies might be. Norbury doesn't want her to be hurt."

"I should hope not! But even so, it's a terrible risk. I ought not allow it in the future."

"Certainly don't allow other men to be alone with Miss Blake. Not for a moment."

"Oh, I'm to trust the rake over all the gentlemen in London?"

"In this case," Carlos said, looking very serious, "yes. I cannot explain why, but I promise you that Norbury is a far safer bet when it comes to Miss Blake's reputation."

"Is it true that he's won every duel he's fought? How many has he fought? Rumors exaggerate."

"Oh, there have been plenty. I've been his second at some of them, so I'd know."

"Lots of aggrieved husbands, are there?"

"And brothers, and fathers..."

"All defending the honor of the ladies he seduced."

"To be honest, they were mostly defending their honor and reputations. Especially the husbands. No one likes to be thought of as a cuckold. But Adrian—I mean Norbury—insists on first blood only. He's not a killer."

"Is it their lives he's truly concerned about?"

"He could have killed every one of them. He's a swordmaster, did you know? As in, he's been recognized as a master, a title very few have earned."

"Really?"

"Oh, yes. He's practiced since a boy."

"But what about pistols? It doesn't take a master to hit a target at twenty paces, does it?"

"No, but again, he's trained, and he's known to be an

excellent shot and absolutely without fear. Not many men choose pistols, knowing the odds."

"You sound as if you've been in a few duels yourself."

"Now and then," he agreed, rather evasively. "In Santo Domingo, where the rules about such things are somewhat...looser."

"And you come to England to do business? I thought Hispaniola was a French possession?" Wasn't England technically at war with France, and thus all its territories?

"At the moment, the Spanish crown has control," he said. "But don't feel that your ignorance is your fault. The flag changes quite frequently, as the powers that be shuffle their chess pieces across the board."

She sensed the frustration in his words. "You prefer it to be French? Or British?"

"I'd prefer it to be Dominican," he replied. "But that is easier said than done. The kings and queens of Europe don't like giving up even the smallest piece of rock. And my island is one of the largest, hence the scuffling."

"Your island, as if it's your private domain?" Poppy asked, amused.

He smiled at her. "Trust me, I know it better than anyone who's claimed it thus far."

"And why is that? What does your family do that you have such knowledge?"

"Oh, we're in the business of imports and exports, and as such, I'm quite familiar with many little ports around the coast," he answered. "But I shouldn't bore a lady with talk of grubby trade."

"I'm not a lady," Poppy informed him, "and as it happens, my stepfather is in trade. I've grubbed in offices and warehouses myself."

"Ah, so that accounts for it," he said quietly.

"Accounts for what?" she asked, suddenly wary. She'd

been snubbed more than once when people learned that her class was not quite the same as her cousin's.

"Your very delightful lack of pretension. Most of the young ladies I encounter in London are about as grounded as a butterfly, with the same level of intelligence. You are different, and I like it."

"I'm not sure if that was a backhanded compliment, but I'll pretend to be grateful to be singled out as a caterpillar among butterflies."

"Never a lowly caterpillar, Miss St. George. A dragon. Formidable and ready to strike whenever a fool wanders too close."

Poppy tried not to be flattered, but it was the first time a man called her a dragon (and with such admiration in his eyes), and she felt as if he might be the first man to have actually seen her as she was.

"You're not afraid I'll breathe fire on you?" she asked.

"I'm known to risk a lot when the reward is worth it."

"And this was the man who clambered up a tree to rescue a cat Rose heard mewing," Poppy said with a laugh.

"How are the kittens?" he asked, seeming to really care about the answer. "Adjusting to life inside walls?"

"Yes, they're settling in well. They even sleep with us."

"Lucky them."

Poppy shot him a narrow-eyed glance, only to be met with a wide-eyed innocent expression that she didn't believe for a moment.

Carlos said, "I had a cat once, back home. She just wandered into the house one day, so I assumed she wanted to stay for a while. Very pretty little black cat."

"What was she named?"

"I christened her Señorita Caterina Gitana de la Guerra. Sadly, she was not enamored of the ocean. I took her on board a few times, because it's good to have a mouser on a ship. But Gitana wailed the whole journey, so I had to give the notion up. She lives out her days at the family estate. Too bad, I would have enjoyed the company. Do you like the ocean?" he asked suddenly.

"No idea. I've never been on anything bigger than a rowboat," Poppy admitted. "And anyway, I'm not a mouser."

He grinned at her. "But you do have claws."

"As my family is all too apt to remind me," she said, looking away.

"I'm not afraid of a few scratches," he replied.

Poppy inhaled, caught by his gaze. It would be easy to like him, if he weren't so vexing. He was an interesting conversationalist, all right, and a good diversion from ordinary...

Diversion. Suddenly Poppy inhaled, and wrenched her elbow out of his hand. "Oh, my goodness, what time is it?"

* * * *

While Carlos did his best to keep Poppy occupied for a little while, Adrian seized his precious few moments alone with Rose.

"Miss Blake, evening becomes you."

"Thank you, sir." Rosalind blushed so much that he could see it in the twilight.

Adrian stepped closer, mindful of the few other people in the area. He started walking a little ways ahead, where a stand of trees divided the path, with the narrower left-hand path heavily shielded from any prying eyes. "Did my gifts find favor with you?" he asked, guiding her to the more secluded location.

"Oh, those anonymous gifts were from you?" she asked with a smile. "Of course I liked them. They were all delightful."

"I worried that you might think they came from another suitor, but I feared that adding my name to them would be folly."

"My mother objected to me having the lilies in my room, but I prevailed." She laughed softly. "Though any flower would have been too suggestive for her taste."

"You have a beautiful smile," he said then, dropping all pretense of a casual conversation. "In fact, all of you is beautiful."

"I've been told so."

"It's true. However, beauty can conceal some ugly souls." He lowered his voice, speaking more seriously. "Rosalind, have you ever asked me about my lineage? My title? How many pounds a year I have?"

By the look on her face, she was rather offended at the idea. "You know I have not. Why should any of that matter to me?"

"You asked me instead about what angered me about society. You asked about my life. What I thought. That makes you unique among all the women I've known."

"I…" Rose stopped, and her expression was full of confusion and even pity. "I'm sorry that's the case, my lord."

"Well, it is, but it's made me very glad to have met you, however unconventional the meeting was." His mind flashed back to the moment he saw her alone on the dance floor, and how his feet were moving toward her even before he'd decided to rescue her.

"It was probably the most exciting night of my life,"

she admitted, "which just proves how dull my life is compared to yours."

"My life's not as carefree as it appears," he told her. "But I'm not here to talk about that."

"What are you here for?"

"For this."

He gently lowered his mouth to hers, expecting her to freeze in surprise. Then a jolt ran through his body when he grazed her lower lip with his tongue, and all thoughts fled. In place of his careful plans for a few teasing kisses, desire flared up and he prodded her mouth open with his tongue, hungry to taste her.

Rose's mouth was hot, her response curious and eager. Her tongue slid against his and she let out a soft moan that made his hands shake, there was so much passion in it.

Out of self-preservation, he closed his mouth and laid kisses on her nose and eyelids and cheeks. He moved to her ear, sucking on one lobe.

Rose's skin burned against his, and he would have her gown off in a minute if he had her truly alone. He heard the rapid beat of her pulse in her neck, and knew that she was just as aroused as he was.

"I thought we were just friends. Do friends kiss like this?" she asked breathlessly.

"If they did, the world would be a much friendlier place," he returned, his heart strangely warm. "And in case it's not clear by now, I intend for us to be much more than friends."

"What do you intend, my lord?" she asked, pulling her head away a few inches, sounding more cautious, back to the society miss whose whole existence hinged on her suitors' intentions.

"Nothing evil," he assured her.

"Says the rake and rogue."

"Rose, I know you shouldn't trust me. Not yet. But do you believe me when I say that I need to meet you again?"

"Yes," she said slowly, her voice full of wariness, but also interest.

"We don't have much time," he noted before catching her chin in his hand, tilting her face up. "Rose, will you let me into your life?"

"I would like to," she said at last, and he didn't realize his heart had stopped until she started it again with those words.

"Then it will happen."

"But I am not entirely free to make that choice," she reminded him. "Even a quarter hour unobserved is difficult to manage. And I think you're not exactly beloved by my parents."

"I'll find a way," he promised. "One more kiss, before your chaperone returns and takes you away." He gathered her into a loose embrace and gave her a kiss designed to stoke more desire instead of satisfying it. At least, that's what the kiss was doing to him. Rose hummed with pleasure as her mouth sought his own, and his mind reeled at the response that stirred in him. He ran his hand up her back, bringing her in closer, ready for more.

Then a voice called Rose's name in the distance.

All too quickly, he released her, silently cursing her companion's devotion.

* * * *

Rosalind was still recovering her breath from that last kiss when Poppy returned in a hurry, her breathing a bit strained, Mr. de la Guerra trailing her by several steps.

"My lord," Poppy said with no trace of deference. "It

seems your friend here lost track of time. But I am ready to take my cousin back to her parents. *Now*."

Dutifully, Adrian stepped away, not before placing Rose's hand back into Poppy's. "Farewell, ladies," he said. "You've reminded me how much I like these gardens."

"I like them too," his friend added. "Though it seems I do have to watch my step."

"Cherish the memory of the evening, then, gentlemen," Poppy snapped. "Because I'm not going to allow this to ever happen again, either to Rose or to me. You may keep your schemes to yourselves. Good night!"

She hustled Rose back toward where the Blakes awaited, but after a moment, she stopped again.

"What is it?" Rose asked. She hadn't noticed her walking stick striking any obstacle. "Is there something in the path?"

"No, but you must tell me. Did he kiss you?" Poppy whispered. "You look like he kissed you. Your cheeks are all flushed! Was it a good kiss? Oh, my lord, he's a rake, of course it was a good kiss."

"Yes, it was, but *please* don't make me talk about it now," Rose begged.

"Later, then. But don't think you'll evade telling me what happened. I hope it was worth it, and I hope we don't get in trouble for this. We'll both be kept under lock and key for the rest of our lives."

Poppy led her back to the table where their family sat, vowing that she'd get the story out of Rosalind when they retired. The girls had only been gone for about twenty minutes or so, though to Rose it seemed like a year had passed. She felt much older, and more bewildered at the world.

Rose listened to her parents' happy talk, and smiled

dutifully when acquaintances stopped by the table. In one case, a man named Mr. Miller approached and asked to dance with Poppy, and she somewhat surprisingly agreed. (He was a frequent caller at the house, and Poppy had deemed him slightly dull but ultimately inoffensive.)

They left Vauxhall when Mrs. Blake announced that she was growing tired, and the still-reeling Rose was happy to return home as well.

Late that same night, Poppy entered their bedroom.

"Are you asleep?" she asked Rose, who was already tucked into bed.

"Not at all."

"Dreaming of your beau?" Poppy asked teasingly.

The voice that answered was morose. "I can't dream if I'm not asleep."

"Daydreaming, then."

"It's not day." Rosalind turned over and tipped her ear toward Poppy.

"What's wrong? Those lilies he sent were quite nice, I thought."

"I'm so stupid," Rosalind suddenly burst out. "I don't even know what's happening. I only met him a week ago, and I can't stop thinking about him. When he met us at Vauxhall it felt like magic. I'm so happy when I hear him say my name. But I don't know what his intentions are. He said he wanted to get to know me, and he kissed me, but he never mentioned actually courting me. Am I mad to expect that he would? What's going on?"

"You're falling in love," Poppy said simply.

"Oh, no."

"Of course you are. And why not? He's a charming, handsome gentleman. And he is courting you. When a man sends flowers and chocolates and finds ways to meet you in dark gardens to kiss you, that's courting."

"Is he? Or is he simply playing? Hynes meant to make fun of me. Who's to say Lord Norbury isn't doing the same? You know the stories about him. Perhaps he's just taking his time to get to the punchline."

"Do you really think that's likely?"

"I don't think it's likely that an aristocrat of his level would seriously court a blind girl. Nor would a rake be interested in a simple little maiden like me."

"Oh, Rose."

"Poppy, I'm not a fool. Even I have heard the stories. Perhaps he just wants a freak for a mistress because it will amuse him."

"Oh, Rose," Poppy repeated sadly. "Don't ever say that." She sat on the edge of the bed, and found her cousin's hand. "If you doubt him, just tell me. I'll make sure he understands that you don't wish his attention."

"But I do wish it," Rosalind burst out again, thoroughly miserable.

"If…" Poppy began hesitantly. "If he did ask you to become a…lover, and not a wife, what would you tell him?"

"I don't know," Rosalind sighed. "I know what I should say."

"But you are attracted to him," Poppy said in understanding. "And you long for a life outside our tiny world, so you would consider becoming a man's mistress, not merely for the excitement, but for the change."

Rosalind was silent for a long moment. Then she asked, "How do you understand so much?"

"I watch the world for the both of us," her companion replied. "And I think a lot. A lot more than any of our parents would approve of."

Rosalind hugged her cousin tight. "I'm sorry to bring all this upon you. I suppose time will sort it out."

"Sooner rather than later, I hope."

Rose sensed that Poppy also had something on her mind. "What is it?"

"I had a letter from my mother," Poppy said. "She told me that the new business is doing very well, with more orders and customers than they intended."

"Isn't that good news?"

"On the surface, yes. But what she's really saying is that she wishes I'd come and work at the shop and the warehouse with them."

Rose didn't like that at all. Losing Poppy when she needed her more than ever? "If the business is doing so well, can't they hire help?"

"My understanding is that they're doing well enough to need more help, but not quite well enough to pay what they'd need to hire the right person to do the extra work."

Now Rose understood. This wasn't a matter of taking on a shopgirl. Poppy was extremely clever and had a good head for figures. Her mother was hoping she'd become the sort of accountant-secretary-*and*-shopgirl, a role that no man would accept and few women would be prepared for. It was the sort of role that required a blood relative, who would do it for love and not the salary.

"Well, you must do as your family wants," Rose said, wishing she had another answer.

"I'm not leaving you," Poppy replied fiercely. "Especially not at this point, with all this…excitement going on. But I do worry about Mama, and how they will manage the business. My stepfather is wary of taking out a loan— it's too likely that one ends up shackled to the terms."

"But we must do something! It isn't right for me to hold you here if you're needed elsewhere."

"I'm needed here more," Poppy said. "If not for me, who would watch out for you? We've got rakehells coming out of the woodwork and a phalanx of suitors spring-ing forth from the shrubbery. What a Season!"

"It's more interesting than I ever guessed it would be," Rose admitted. "But *interesting* is just another word for *confusing*."

Poppy kissed her cousin good-night, promising that the next day would be better. "Everything will get sorted one way or another."

Rose just hoped she was right.

Chapter 14

THE NEXT MORNING, CARLOS WAS sitting in Adrian's very comfortable parlor. Overnight, the weather had turned British, drizzling cold rain on the city. A fire had been laid to fight off the drafts of the big house. On mornings like these, Carlos missed the warm breezes off the ocean, and the palm trees surrounding the house.

He stared into the fireplace, the flames reflecting against his eyes, turning them gold.   Anyone watching would have thought that the man had a lot on his mind.

In fact, he had only one thing on his mind, and that thing was Poppy St. George.

That girl had spirit. He liked the way she snapped back at every barb. He liked how fiercely she protected her cousin. He liked that her name was Poppy. He liked that her lower lip stuck out when she was thinking hard.

In short, Poppy St. George had shot Carlos in the heart before he had a chance to defend himself, and the result was that every time he tried to think of something else, he found himself picturing her, laughing at some comment, or regarding him with a quizzical smile.

It was damned inconvenient. He had real problems to consider. Not just helping Adrian to counter the gang of idiots working to ruin a girl for fun, but also the ordinary problems of his family's various business interests and a few other matters that he kept more or less private, since they were not entirely legal.

Then again, perhaps Poppy St. George was not his problem after all. The previous evening, she'd turned from kitten to dragon the moment she realized that they'd been talking longer than planned. Carlos immediately told her that it wasn't intentional (he'd completely lost track of time and in fact had no idea that they'd moved quite far away from where Adrian and Rosalind had gone). But Poppy clearly considered it a nefarious plot and rushed back to her cousin. Carlos could barely keep up with her —who knew a woman wearing an evening gown could even move that fast?

When he and Adrian left the women in the gardens, he didn't look back at her. Either Poppy would be looking at him with those searing eyes, which would unnerve him... or she would not be, which would shatter his ego.

Just then, Adrian entered the room, still in his dressing gown, looking very much like he hadn't slept. Behind him, a servant entered, bearing a silver tray loaded down with yet more silver, including a large coffeepot. Carlos realized he hadn't eaten or drank anything yet, and his stomach growled loudly enough for the others to hear.

"Breakfast for both of us, then," Adrian told the servant.

"Yes, milord." The servant put the tray down and slipped away.

Adrian poured coffee for Carlos, and then another for himself. "God, I need this."

Carlos agreed wordlessly, taking a sip. Adrian always had excellent coffee at his houses (indeed, he had excellent everything).

"How did you sleep?" Adrian asked.

"Better than you did, I'm guessing."

"Lot on my mind," his friend muttered. "Rose mentioned her parents don't like me much."

"Shocking, that."

"My own reputation is one thing—I'll talk them around on that. I'm more concerned about the other suitors with less honorable intentions."

"Less honorable than yours? Protecting the girl from men like Evans is all well and good. But nothing about meeting Rosalind in Vauxhall Gardens and getting her alone is very protective."

"I'm going to marry her."

"Excuse me?" Carlos asked. If Adrian had announced he was abdicating his title and walking to India to live at an ashram for the rest of his life, that would be less surprising than what he just said.

"Rosalind Blake is going to be the next Viscountess Norbury."

"Did you have her alone longer than I thought?"

"Jesus Christ, I didn't seduce her last night." Adrian looked annoyed, then his expression shifted to something Carlos had never seen on his face before. "I want her. I mean, I want to have her in my life."

"And your family and the *ton* and all those judging little magpies who write gossip in the newspapers will accept her as a viscountess?"

"Why not?"

Carlos sighed and held up one hand. He put up a finger for every objection. "She has no title herself. She's not particularly wealthy. She has no land. She's blind. And she's the subject of one of the nastiest wagers I can remember."

Adrian held up his own hand. "She's intelligent. She's talented. She's beautiful. She's honest. And she makes me happy whenever I see her."

"Well, that's a good list in my view, but I was talking about society, which is not as open-minded as I am. And you're the one who has to live with the consequences."

"No, society has to live with my reality," Adrian retorted, sounding very much like the aristocrat he was. "But before I ask to marry her, I want to get this whole issue with the wager sorted out. I'm not having Rose plagued by any scandal on her wedding day."

"The problem of Rosalind Blake's would-be ruiners can be solved very simply," said Carlos. "If it were up to me, I'd just arrange it so that one or two of them turned up naked and bound with rope in some public square with a rose jammed into their mouth...well, the others would get the idea quickly enough."

Adrian voted that idea down, unfortunately, saying that it was too violent and would draw even more attention.

"Do it right, and it won't," Carlos countered.

"We're in England. We have to be subtle."

"Fine, we can grab Evans and the whole list and drop them into the Thames. No one will ever find them, and anyone else involved in the whole mess will quietly walk away."

"That's not subtle."

"Efficient, though."

"It would be best if the bookmaker just canceled the wager altogether," Adrian said. "Declare it null and void."

"He never would. That's death for a bookmaker, to arbitrarily pull a bet off the books."

"It's been done."

"Only when there's obvious signs of tampering. Remember when it came out that the jockey was dosing Lord Randell's best horse a few years ago? All the wagers on its races were pulled."

"Because the news of the dosing was public," Adrian agreed with a thoughtful frown.

"And that won't work for us, because we don't want anything about your Miss Blake to get more public than it already is."

"But perhaps we can take the wind out of the sails a bit," Adrian said, getting an idea. "After all, we know several names of the men who are involved. If I call upon them privately, I can make it quite clear that they ought to correct any misapprehensions about their dealings with Rosalind. Because if they don't, I'll challenge them."

"That might work. None of those men are paragons of courage. They'll say whatever they have to to avoid a duel."

"Then let's get to it."

"Breakfast first," Carlos said, seeing two servants come in with trays loaded with good-smelling food. "I never intimidate people on an empty stomach."

Chapter 15

THE YOUNG RAKE SHOWED AN extraordinary ability to charm people and make his way into the private quarters of any woman he chose to pursue. At the moment, he'd selected Poppy as the object of his affection, largely because she was dangling a long piece of fabric scrap from her hand, drawing it along the floor to entice the cat onward.

"Come along, Ralph, yes, here you go! Oh, so fierce! You will be formidable when you're older, yes you will."

Poppy's cooing might have surprised others, but Rose had experienced the softer side of Poppy's nature. She was sharp and flinty around most people, but turned into fleece when confronted with animals, children, or those in need.

The girls were currently in the parlor, after eating a light breakfast and preparing for what seemed the inevitable onslaught of suitors for Rose.

After the fateful evening in Vauxhall Gardens, Rosalind had worked hard to give herself a new outlook. She wouldn't pine after Viscount Norbury, who had not called on her since (even though he still sent an anonymous bouquet every morning). She certainly wouldn't wait around, for she had correctly assessed the likelihood of any sort of legitimate association with him.

None.

Perhaps one of these other men who'd been calling on the Blake house would turn out to be more interesting than those she'd met so far. Apart from Mr. Evans, who had not returned after the fiasco of a carriage ride, the others continued to show a degree of interest. Rose expected that a few of them would arrive when it came time for proper visiting hours.

However, that did not seem to be the case. In contrast to the last several days, Alice was not kept running to and from the front door to announce callers, because none came.

"Not that I'm complaining," Poppy said at one point, "but I was expecting to have to glare at some gentlemen today."

"Perhaps a new blind girl has come to town and captured their fancy," Rose joked. "If so, I wish her joy of them. But this *is* a little dull, just sitting around waiting. What if we get a carriage to Fabric Row?"

"Good idea!" Poppy answered.

So that was what the girls did. With one of the footmen to act as a sort of bodyguard, chaperone, and pack mule, they wandered in and out of shops to find new cloth for their summer dresses. Poppy noted a few items that her stepfather might carry, and Rose enjoyed touching all the bolts of cotton and wool and silk. There was such a pleasure in the feel of beautiful things. She almost felt like her old self, just happy to exist in a little world of friends and family. Not worrying about being left alone on a dance floor or trapped in a carriage or being rescued by a rake.

Several hours later, they returned to the house with enough fabric and lace and notions to outfit an army (a very feminine army, to be sure). Rose's mother expressed approval of the choices, since she trusted Poppy's taste and Rose's good sense.

Her father made the usual noises of concern over the cost, but Rose could tell he was only going through the motions. Mr. Blake kept a firm hand on the family finances, and extravagance would never be tolerated.

"Let's get everything upstairs," Poppy said to one of the servants. "I'll show you where I want it put."

She led the way up, accompanied by an excited Mrs. Blake, who wanted to know if Poppy was going to use the latest Parisian designs (fashion was apparently immune to the continuing hostilities between the countries).

Since Rose and her father had a few precious moments alone, she hesitantly broached the concept of offering Poppy a companion's wages.

"*Pay* her?" Mr. Blake asked in horror. "As if she were some sort of hired girl and not your very own cousin? That would be insulting to Poppy. We are delighted to support her as part of the household and I daresay she eats better and sleeps better than many."

That was undoubtably true, for Poppy's mother had accepted a much lower standard of living when she chose to marry a man in trade, moving to a cramped dwelling above the new shop. But she had done it happily, with a husband she truly loved.

"It's not for Poppy herself," Rose explained. "She'd pass the earnings on to her mother and stepfather. The new shop is succeeding, but costs are exceeding the income for the moment…or so I understand." Rose was not versed in matters of business at all. "I'd hate to think that Poppy is helping me more than her own parents."

Her father held silent, thinking. Then he said, "I see. Perhaps something can be done. Let me look into the matter. After all, it would be terrible to lose Poppy. She is such a great comfort to us all."

"Thank you, Papa!" Rose hugged him, ever grateful that she had such a caring family.

* * * *

Upstairs, Poppy directed the servants where to put all the items they'd purchased that day. She was excited to make new dresses, and she knew exactly what to do for Rose's gowns. Her ideas for her own wardrobe were a bit more muddled.

She picked up the letter from the top of the chest where Alice had placed it earlier that day. Recognizing Heather's handwriting, she quickly broke the seal.

Dear Poppy,

Life with my uncle is getting worse than ever. He's always pestering me to look pretty and proper when his old cronies come to the house for a visit, as if it matters what they think of me or I of them! They play cards in the parlor till all hours and Uncle is losing every time, I'm sure. He looks terrible in the mornings—not that I see him till practically noon, for he is no early riser. Whisky is certainly involved, and I do not like it.

I cannot wait until my birthday. It will be better than any of the previous twenty birthdays, for my gift will be freedom. Glorious freedom, when I'll have control of my fortune and my future. I fully intend to move out and rent rooms somewhere so that I can be a spinster in peace! Perhaps near Wildwood Hall, so I can call upon Mrs. Bloomfield and borrow all the books in her library. I have decided that my family shall be three cats and two dogs. Possibly rabbits, but no men! They are more trouble than any devil. (Mr. Blake excepted, of course. And your step-father, Mr. St. George, who was so nice when I met him. And I suppose the Duke of Lyon. And his friend Mr. Kemble, who was so helpful during that whole nasty business. But that is the absolute end of the list.)

How I whine! Forgive me, but I am quite sour at the world at the moment. I should have waited to write letters, that is certain. Don't read this one aloud to Rose, please. I never want to distress her, and this is unpleasant talk. I shall write a letter to her that is all sunshine and gentleness, I promise. But not today! Today I am clouds and storm.

Please write to me and tell me what is going on. I've heard Rose has a thousand suitors. Can it be true? I hope so, for Rose deserves it. I think she is the sweetest of us (certainly I will not claim that title). Tell me all the news.

Much love,

Heather

Poppy folded the letter back up, staring thoughtfully into the distance. Heather was far away, and it had been too long since she and Rose had a proper visit. Perhaps something could be arranged. It would be good to have Heather about—though she claimed to be sour and stormy, Poppy knew her to be a fun and adventurous girl, always ready with a laugh and able to enliven any room she was in. Her uncle must be acting crotchety indeed to make Heather so upset.

Poppy was very fortunate to have Mr. Blake as her uncle. In fact, she was lucky in her whole family. Her stepfather was a kind and generous man, and her parents clearly adored each other. She was lucky that her aunt and uncle had offered her the position of Rose's companion, which allowed both families to support each other in their way. Poppy's and Rose's mothers were sisters, and it was also fortunate that the decision of one of them to marry a tradesman did not impair their relationship. Poppy knew that some families of the upper classes had disowned members who went into trade or married into trade.

How silly, she thought. Trade was essential, and the upper classes relied upon it to get everything they prized so much. Secretly, Poppy suspected that jealousy was the root of the matter, for some in the growing middle class were wealthier than the gentry who despised them. Poppy's father was not among those *nouveau riche*—not yet! But she had a comfortable life, surrounded by loving family, and she did not want any more than that.

Then why did she dream of going to new places, different places, and living a very different life than the one offered to her? It felt disrespectful to her family to even think of it, and such ideas left Poppy feeling like an ungrateful brat.

Moments later, Mr. Blake escorted Rose into the room, smiling at Poppy as he helped Rose to a chair. "Well, should I expect to see all new gowns by supper?"

"You mean summer, not supper!" Rose laughed. "Poppy's a seamstress, not a sorceress. You'll see the new gowns by *summer*."

"And I'm sure you'll both look lovely in them. I hope you two will relax before supper. All that running around London's shops must exhaust a young lady."

"No more than arguing in Chancery exhausts a gentleman," Poppy returned gamely.

"Ah, it tires me out more than I care to admit. I look forward to the day I can finish this case and leave the city. It will be good for all of us," he added with a slight frown.

Poppy wondered if he'd heard more rumors about Lord Norbury...such as a rumor that the viscount managed to be alone with Rose at Vauxhall for a little too long.

But Mr. Blake simply said he'd see them downstairs in the dining room, and left.

Before Poppy could mention Heather's letter, Alice poked her head in conspiratorially. "A box for Miss Blake arrived this afternoon." She placed it carefully on the table, as if it might hold an adder. The box was wooden, stamped with lettering in one of the languages used in India, though Poppy was not able to tell exactly which one. She'd seen similar script on some of the shipments of cotton and silk at the warehouse.

Alice went on, "Flowers are one thing, but this package looked a little more…special. I didn't want Mrs. Blake to order it burned on the rubbish heap."

"Good thinking, Alice." Poppy reached for a folded paper on top of it. "There's a note this time. Shall I read it, Rose?" she asked as the maid backed out of the room.

"I suppose," Rose replied, clearly intrigued.

Poppy cleared her throat, reading, "'I regret not being able to visit you in person in the past few days, and I hope the gifts provided some enjoyment in the absence of my own charming personality. Today's gift is more practical. I hope that it will be of use to you tomorrow evening.'"

"He's quite confident," Poppy concluded with her own assessment. "I wonder what he means by tomorrow evening. We've got no plans at all."

"Let's find out what's inside," Rose begged.

Poppy pulled off the lid. She reached in, encountering a softness she didn't expect.

"What is it?" Rose asked.

"It's…soft." She pulled it out. "It's cashmere. Not dyed at all, just the raw cashmere. It's lovely." She couldn't keep a note of jealousy out of her voice, for she recognized that this was cashmere of extremely high quality, such that only the rich could dream of buying.

"A wrap?"

"I think so. Yes, here. Try it on." Poppy draped it around Rose's shoulders, seeing how flushed her cousin got, and also how the ivory tone of the wrap made her skin look brighter and more aglow.

"He's not a skinflint, I'll give him that," Poppy said. "It looks lovely on you."

"It feels lovely," Rose agreed, happiness written all over her face. "But I still don't understand why he thought I'd have a specific use for it." She brought the soft woven material up to her nose. "Mmm, it smells of sandalwood. So does he."

"Oh, Lord, I don't need to know what he smells like!" Poppy said, unaccountably embarrassed to learn such an intimate detail of a man. "And until you learn more, I'd suggest hiding the wrap. If your mother thought we'd actually paid for that today, she'd never let us go to the high street again."

Poppy folded the wrap up and put it back in the box, then stashed the box under her bed.

At supper that evening, all was surprisingly normal. Mr. and Mrs. Blake chattered happily about their days. Poppy enjoyed hearing them talk because each was so genuinely interested in the other's life. She prayed she'd someday find someone who'd be half so interested in her.

After eating, the women moved to the drawing room to relax for a while. Mr. Blake would smoke a single cigar before joining them—even without a male dinner companion, he kept to the rules, which included never offending ladies with the presence of smoke.

Alice entered again with another message on the tray. "Excuse me, ma'am," she said to Mrs. Blake, "but this just arrived, and I thought it might be urgent."

Mrs. Blake opened it instantly. "Oh! We have been invited to a ball tomorrow night at Lady Worthington's." This was both a surprise and compliment, since Lady Worthington was known to host some of the most extravagant parties in London. Invitations were highly sought after.

"How did we manage that?" Rose asked.

"There's a note included that says she heard that you were the hit of Lady Selby's musicale."

"An exaggeration."

"Who cares?" Poppy interjected. "She wants you to come, and her parties are always talked about."

"But you said earlier you'll spend the evening with your mother," Rose noted. "So I'll stay home."

"Ugh, no. This is a Lady Worthington party. You have to go! You might never get a chance again. Your mother can chaperone."

Mrs. Blake made a mournful sound. "Unfortunately, I've got that event at Sir Edward's tomorrow night. It's been planned for weeks. And Rose's papa is working late on his case, so he won't even be home."

"We have to find someone!" Poppy pleaded. "What about Lady Sara? If she's going to tonight's event anyway, she can chaperone Rose."

"That's true," Mrs. Blake said, brightening. "I'd hate for Rose to miss an opportunity to meet a *proper* suitor."

Poppy couldn't ignore her aunt's look toward Rose, who remained blissfully ignorant. Obviously, Lord Norbury hadn't charmed the Blakes even though he'd charmed their daughter. Poppy bit her lip, afraid that things were spiraling out of control, and Rose would be the one to get hurt.

Chapter 16

LADY SARA MONROE WAS AN acquaintance of Mrs. Blake and Mrs. St. George. She was uncommonly pretty, good-hearted, and had the attention span of a goldfish. She wore some of the most fabulous gowns ever to appear at *ton* parties, and thus was a frequent guest at large affairs. It was said that she dressed as daringly as the late Duchess of Devonshire, but (thank goodness) spent her money much more carefully.

Mrs. Blake wrote to her first thing in the morning to ask if she could chaperone Rose at the party. A few hours later Lady Sara sent back an enthusiastic reply that she was going herself already and of course it would be a pleasure to take Rose along. *I shall stop by in my carriage around eight*, she said in conclusion.

So Rose was going to this party, despite not knowing about it a day before. She tried to be excited, but she was mostly bewildered.

"What should I wear?" she asked her cousin that afternoon.

"I think your pink silk would be best," Poppy replied. "It's been warm today and wool would be insufferable at any sort of indoor gathering."

"Oh, should I not use my cashmere wrap, then?" Rose

asked sadly. She'd loved the feel of the wrap when she tried it the night before. It was lightweight but somehow buttery, and felt utterly luxurious against her skin. Of course Adrian would have thought of that—he'd chosen a gift that she didn't need to see to appreciate.

That evening, after Poppy helped Rose dress, they moved downstairs to the parlor.

Mrs. Blake left for her event, reminding Rose at least three times to enjoy herself and be careful of any and all men.

"Especially Lord Norbury," she added unnecessarily. "If he tries to dance with you, you must refuse him."

"Should I wait for Mr. Hynes to ask again?" Rose returned dryly. "At least Lord Norbury didn't leave me halfway through."

Mrs. Blake couldn't carry on the argument, since her carriage was at the door. She kissed Rose, saying, "Just don't do anything you'll regret."

"Yes, Mama."

Soon after that, Poppy also left, in a hired cab that would take her to her parents' home. "Your mother's fears aside, do be careful, Rose," she cautioned. "I'm not afraid of Norbury, exactly, but I just feel like something's going to happen. Too many social circles are crossing, and you know how some people hate that. I'm worried."

"It's a party, I'll be chaperoned, and I won't dance with anyone I don't trust. Now go. Your mother will think we're keeping you prisoner here."

Poppy left, and Rose waited for Lady Sara, expecting the sweet but sometimes absent-minded woman to be late.

However, Lady Sara was actually early. She greeted Rose with affectionate kisses and much cooing over the kittens, who were lounging in the parlor.

"Come, darling, we must be off. Tonight's party will

be a rout, and it will take all our prayers to get to the door before midnight."

Thankfully, the reality was a little less horrible, though a line of carriages in front of the door to Lady Worthington's townhome was long and slow-moving. Sara counted them off, and included a running commentary of the names and outfits of everyone she could see walking up the steps.

"Oh, that's Lady Markham. She looks just darling in that green silk. I should get a green silk gown. A light green, not a dark green, obviously. I've got two dark greens. I could have little flowers beaded on at the bottom. Or maybe a huge green organza bow at the waist. Or peacock feathers in my hair. What do you think?"

"Why not all three?" Rose suggested mildly.

"You're a genius. Of course that's the best way to do it. Did Mr. and Mrs. Pettengill bring their *dogs*? They did! Oh, this will be pure chaos," Sara said happily.

Chaos was a good way to describe the party. There seemed to be a thousand guests, and there were certainly a thousand flowers, because Rose could smell them all, plus the peculiar scent of sweaty bodies in close quarters. She instantly questioned whether she should have come at all, but perhaps Adrian was going to meet her here. He must have arranged for Lady Worthington to invite her.

However, the first hour passed and he never appeared.

The second hour passed, and he never appeared.

Other people did, and many of them approached Rose and Sara to ask for an introduction or to request a dance. Rose consented to the introductions (via Sara) but politely refused the dances, the memory of the last time she danced with a man who asked too fresh in her mind.

So she sat there quietly, while Sara and her circle of friends chattered away. She listened in vain for any mention of Adrian, but if he was at the party, none of the women had noticed. Rose wanted to enjoy herself, but the warnings of her mother and Poppy rang in her ears. Perhaps she shouldn't be out at a party like this.

"You look a bit faded, Miss Blake," a gentleman named Sir Richard said to her then. "Would you care to take a stroll in the gardens?"

"No, thank you," Rose replied, thinking that the last thing she needed was to be found alone with another man, this time one she didn't even know.

He was persistent, but Sara eventually noticed and shooed him away.

"Some men really should not be allowed out," she said. "Really! How many times must he hear that his attention is not wanted?"

"Is there a quieter room?" Rose asked. "I may have a headache."

She did not have a headache, but she had been entirely overwhelmed by the crowd and noise and the endless stimuli, picking out bits of conversations while trying to ignore the musicians in the other room, and yet more men asking her to dance or accept a drink or a stroll in the gardens. Having learned her lesson before, Rose declined all of the requests that would take her away from Sara's view. The result was that she didn't have very much fun, and she missed Poppy's presence. She half hoped Adrian would be there and come over to her. But Sara did not mention him, Rose was afraid to ask about him, and he was probably doing something else more interesting tonight anyway.

"You poor thing. Come with me, just down this hallway," Sara said, drawing Rosalind forward by the hand.

Rose allowed Sara to lead her away from the ballroom into a quieter, cooler passageway. She heard a door open, then Sara drew her inside a room that was blessedly calm, the only sound being the soft rustle of the skirts of other ladies taking advantage of the retiring room.

"All that noise and heat, it's no surprise you're over-whelmed. Here, drink this," Sara said, placing a glass of something cool into Rose's hands. "I'll come back in a few moments to see if you're feeling better."

She left, and Rose took a cautious sip of the beverage, which turned out to be water infused with lemon and orange. The sharp citrus notes were a welcome counterpoint to the floral perfumed air of the ballroom.

Rose sat, breathing slowly. Was it foolish of her to come to this event at all? Considering that she was afraid to accept even an invitation to dance, there was little point in her attending. But the facts were simply that Hynes's earlier trick had burned itself into her brain, and she feared that it could happen again. And if it did, there was no chance that she'd be saved by someone like Adrian the next time. After all, there was only one Adrian.

A thin sigh escaped her at the thought of him. Where was he? Not at this party, certainly. Why then had he sent the cashmere wrap, with the heavy hint that she'd want it tonight? Was her invitation to this party just a coincidence? Did she misunderstand Adrian's intentions?

Rose shook her head. She must have, and no wonder. She was obviously too sheltered and naive to catch the undercurrents of their exchanges. She was very silly to think that his continued attention actually meant anything. He lived in a different world than her, and if Rose were smart, she'd return to her own little world as fast as possible.

Some time later, Sara entered the retiring room, going immediately to Rose (her perfume heralded her approach by several paces). "Rose, darling, are you not feeling any better?"

"Yes and no," Rose said. "But I have decided that I'd better go home."

"Oh, that's such a shame! There's going to be some massive surprise later, so they say."

"It sounds exciting, but I doubt I'll be able to appreciate it." Rose felt better, having resolved to leave the surprises of high society alone. Let others enjoy them, people who had the freedom to do so. "Can you help me to the foyer where I can call for a carriage?"

"I've got mine, dear!"

"But it will take an hour to retrieve, and anyway I want you to stay and enjoy the party."

"I can't send you off in a cab alone...can I?" Sara sounded quite confused about what she ought to do or even what she felt like doing.

"Get me into a carriage and give the street direction. I'll be just fine. It's not a long ride."

Sara escorted Rose to the giant doors of Lady Worthington's home, which had been propped open to allow the cool night air inside. A footman standing at the ready listened to Lady Sara's request for a carriage to take Miss Blake home, and he then dashed outside to hail one of the hired carriages in the nearest lane, where they always hovered at the time of a party.

Rose listened to what sounded like an accident on the street—men yelling and horses neighing.

"What's going on?" she asked, concerned.

"There's a bit of a jam-up with the carriages. Silly drivers, they all want the fare! Oh, one's edged ahead of the mess, that's wonderful. Just fancy, a carriage driver who can actually drive a carriage!"

"That's a change," Rose commented, having suffered through many bumpy rides through the cobbled streets of

London.

The footman returned. "Right this way, ladies. Carriage is waiting."

Arm in arm, Sara led Rose to the street, and the footman held the door open. Rose climbed in, feeling the side of the door and the leather seat.

"Comfortable, dear?" Sara asked. Then she called up Rose's street and number to the driver. "Got that? The household will pay the fare when you drop her off. Now take care, Rose! I do hope you feel better."

"I shall. You enjoy the rest of the party, and do write to me about the surprise."

"Absolutely, darling! Good night!"

The carriage rolled away, leaving Sara's cheerful farewell behind. Rose sighed as she sagged back into the seat.

The carriage continued on through the city, the driver taking turns into this street or that as he navigated the crowds. At last, the carriage slowed and came to a stop. Rose waited for the driver to open the door, knowing she'd have to explain that she was blind and ask for him to escort her all the way to the front door of the house. She never liked to ask (not that she usually had to. Rose could count the number of times she'd ridden alone on one hand).

The door opened, and Rose put her hand out as she leaned forward. The driver took her hand…and kissed it.

"I was worried you'd be at that party till dawn," a warm voice said.

"Adrian!" Rose gasped, withdrawing her hand in surprise. "What's going on? Where's the driver?"

"I am the driver, darling."

"You drove me home?"

"In a manner of speaking. Actually, I drove you to *my*

home. Care to come in?"

Rose inhaled. This was an invitation to ruin. Spending a night with a man, without any oversight whatsoever? She'd never be allowed among society again.

"Or I can drive you to your house," Adrian went on. "Drop you off at the door, and you go in, no one the wiser. Up to you, Rose."

Rose felt multiple futures spreading out before her, and in a flash she knew which way she chose to take. She put her hand out once more, allowing Adrian to take it.

"Thank you," she said. "I would like to come in."

Chapter 17

ROSE TOOK AN UNSTEADY BREATH as Adrian helped her from the carriage. Her heartbeat was already rising, just thinking about the incredible risk she was taking.

Adrian ran his fingers along her arm, which was covered in the cashmere wrap. "I'm glad you wore it."

"Well, you told me to."

"No, I suggested it because I thought you might like it, and you should have things you can enjoy. But you certainly didn't have to wear it."

She sensed Adrian's presence then, and his unique combination of sandalwood and spices. His arms embraced her, surrounding her with warmth.

Rosalind reveled in the feeling, but tried to keep some sense about her. "I thought we were going inside your lair, I mean, your house?"

"Yes, indeed. This way to my lair." He put an arm to her elbow and guided her up steps, estimating the count to the stairs leading to his door.

Once inside, Rose felt the enfolding silence of the place.

"Servants have been given the night off," he explained. "Not that they'd mention anything if they were here, but everyone deserves time off now and again."

"Adrian, are you sure about this? It's not exactly a revelation that I'm an unmarried woman, and thus should not be alone with you, or any man, ever—"

He put a finger to her lips. "Trust me. I've arranged it all. No one saw me drive the carriage, or rather no one would recognize me. A friend of mine will vow that I'm somewhere else at this moment, if need be."

"But I've been discouraged from even talking with you."

"Ironic. Now that I finally decide I want to rejoin polite society, they throw obstacles in my path."

"What do you mean?"

"Shush, Rose, we don't have much time."

"Time for what?"

"For this." He leaned forward to kiss her. Rosalind was beguiled anew by the sensations. She might be every time he touched her. He seemed hellbent on distracting her from asking any more questions, for he was tantalizing her with his hands and mouth.

"What are you planning to do?" she whispered when she thought to speak.

"Well, first I'm going to ask you for a favor."

"Which is what, exactly?"

"Would you sing for me?"

Rose assumed she misheard. "Excuse me? You spirited me away for a *concert?*" And here she'd thought he intended to ravish her. (Not to mention that she was rather hoping he would.)

"I can't get your voice out of my head," he told her. "I was hoping you'd take pity on me and let me hear it again."

"Perform a song, here in your house?"

"Not perform. Just sing. Your voice gives me chills."

"Really?" She couldn't help but laugh. "As if I scare

you?"

"It scares me to think I've heard you sing once but might never hear you again. You could raise me from the dead with your voice, Rose. No, I'm not being facetious now. I mean it. When you sang, you made me feel... alive."

Rose inhaled, shaken by the confession.

Adrian led her to a room on the ground floor, a smaller room by the sound of it, or otherwise the walls and windows were draped with enough fabric to cushion any stray noises.

"This is my reading room," he explained. "Comfortable couch and chairs, very secluded. Will this do?"

"For a song? Yes, perfectly."

He guided her to a spot on the floor, and told her that he'd sit on the couch about ten feet in front of where she stood. "I haven't got a piano. Yet. Or any instrument, really. Do you need something for...I don't know, tuning? I remember when your cousin played a note for you at that recital."

Rose shook her head, surprised he even noticed that little detail. "I'm going to sing a cappella and solo. It doesn't matter what key I begin in. And I've always had good pitch."

"Then I'll just sit down and shut up," Adrian said.

So Rose sang. She warmed her voice up with a favorite aria that Maestro Valdi had declared suited her range perfectly. Rose liked the lower alto registers, and she kept her volume lower than usual, since the concert felt so clandestine, even if they were alone in the house.

There was something nerve-racking in performing for an unseen audience of one. Rose was used to performing for her family, gathered in the drawing room in their usual seats, with their usual supportive attention. Rose could always sense their presences because she was so familiar with them.

But Adrian was different. The room was different, the acoustics were different, everything was different. Rose knew he was sitting down, because she heard the creak of the wood and rustle of fabric when he did so. But she had little sense of what else was in the room, only that it was small enough that her voice did not echo.

And she did not know what he thought of her music. He was listening in total silence. But was it attentive or bored? Did he regret asking for this? Was he less impressed this time, having built up his memory of the first time he heard her sing into an impossible perfection?

She finished the song, and inhaled deeply, getting her breath back.

"Did you...like that?" she asked into the deep silence.

Then he stood, and walked over to her, his hands resting tightly on her torso, just under the bust of her dress. His fingertips just grazed her rib cage, and stayed there.

"Gorgeous," he said, his voice a little rough. "Sing something else. Please."

"Right now? You don't want to sit again?"

"I want to feel the music."

Rose swallowed, and then took a deep breath, from the belly, preparing for the next song.

She let the first notes out slowly, tenderly. This was a much more challenging song, with long, long notes she had to hold until the very end, when she could play with a demi-quaver and a flourish as she got the whim.

She heard Adrian breathing, and felt the absolute concentration of his attention on her. No one besides her instructors had ever listened to her this closely before. Rose was acutely aware of the faint vibrations generated by her singing, her lungs swelling, pushing her ribs out...and there were Adrian's hands to register the feeling.

"Keep singing," he ordered softly. He kissed her neck, and again Rose was more aware of the physical effects of singing than she'd ever been. The way her throat opened and her lungs filled. The way the vibrato in her vocal cords rippled through her body. The way her breath came and went, inhaling the cool air of the room and exhaling the same air as music warmed by her own flesh.

On the last note, she maintained her breath as long as she could, spinning out the tone to a final, lingering sound. But just before the note ended, Adrian lowered his mouth to hers, and the music became a kiss.

Rose was lost. Music was passion given sound, and the intimacy of a private concert was more than enough to raise her heart rate and send her imagination running rampant.

And now her imagination had to bow out, replaced by the far more sensuous reality of being in Adrian's arms, feeling his mouth on her skin, and listening to his breath as he ran his hands over her.

"My lord…"

"Adrian," he corrected. "You've said it before, and we're much too close to use formal address between each other now."

"Are we? Close, I mean?"

"You think I ask just any woman to sing for me, going to absurd lengths to get her into a place where only I can hear?"

"I'm sure I'm not the first woman you've gone to absurd lengths to get alone."

"But you are the first I've begged to let me hear as you sing." His fingertip gently brushed her cheek. "The first I can't stop dreaming of."

"Dreaming?" Rose asked, surprised.

He paused, perhaps embarrassed by the confession. Then he said, "Every night."

"So you didn't just compromise my reputation to hear me sing?"

"No, I'm intending to do more than that. You have two choices, Rose."

"What are they?"

"I can take you home now, possibly compromised but still a virgin. Or I can take you upstairs, where you will very definitely be compromised and you won't be a virgin for much longer."

"It almost sounds like you want me to leave."

"God, no. But I want you to decide for yourself."

Go back to her old life, or experience something entirely new? What sort of choice was that?

Rose took a slow breath, then said, "Please take me upstairs."

He led her up a curving flight of stairs, the marble making their footsteps echo in the foyer. As Rose moved deeper into the house, she felt as if she'd never emerge in the real world again. Or perhaps she would, but she wouldn't be the same person.

"This is the door to my rooms," he said at last, stopping.

"Well, then you'd better open it," Rose replied, trying to keep her tone light when in fact her heart was hammering with anticipation.

"I'm rushing you," he said then. "I'm used to taking what I want, but you're different…"

"Adrian, if you try to put me off one more time—" Rose leaned into him and put her hands very firmly on the lapels of his jacket, keeping him in front of her. Then she raised her mouth and found his.

The kiss betrayed her impatience, and her hunger.

Rose was done with sitting quietly while others decided her life. At least for this moment, she was going to take what *she* wanted.

And she wanted Adrian. She wanted to know how he felt to touch, how it would be to lie with him in a bed and have nothing between them.

Adrian responded with a hunger of his own, and Rose grew wild as he deepened the kiss to a new level of need, breathing in faster as she fell into the desire blooming through her body.

"Open the door," Rose gasped, and he did, pushing it inward and taking her through.

"Bed is over here," he told her, then simply picked her up and carried her there, setting her down on what she could tell was a massive bed. Rose found it amazingly comfortable, with mounds of pillows to cushion her weight.

Adrian put one knee on the bed, and she heard the sound of him pulling his jacket off, then the soft whisper of linen as his shirt followed.

He moved toward her, taking her hands and drawing them to his torso. "Touch me," he instructed, his voice low and laced with passion.

She ran her fingers over his chest, feeling the texture and temperature of him, learning how he was shaped and how his muscles curved and rippled under her touch. She strove to memorize every moment, certain that she'd never experience this again. Then she moved her hands to his neck and his face, pulling him toward her.

"I like this," she told him, "I like feeling you and knowing how you're shaped. People have told me you're handsome, and I don't know what that means anymore, but I know I like to touch you and kiss you and smell you."

"I just wish you could see how beautiful you are, Rose," he said, his breath against her cheek. "But I'm going to make you feel beautiful tonight."

"You always do," she whispered.

"This way will be new." Adrian knelt between her legs, and his hands moved under her skirt, pushing the fabric up to her thighs, exposing her skin to the cooler air. She shivered involuntarily.

"Scared?" he asked. "The carriage is just outside. I can still stop this and take you home, right now."

"Don't you dare." If Rose was going to be compromised, she wasn't going to miss the most important part of the process. "I want to know what I've been missing."

She could actually feel the smile on his face when he replied, "Thank God."

He knelt down lower, then Rose felt his mouth on her inner thigh, his tongue hot, and the faintest hint of stubble grazing her skin. She gasped at the sensation, never having felt anything like it before.

His attention moved slowly upward, and before Rose could even think to be shocked, she was under a spell, her body reacting to the most intimate touch she'd felt from anyone.

"That's your tongue," she gasped.

He gave an *mmm-hmm* of assent, the sound rippling against her body. Rose moaned as he continued to lick her there, bringing up entirely new feelings of pleasure and need. She allowed him everything, following every instruction to move or lift her hips or tell him to speed up or slow down.

Only after she was whimpering, aching for release, did he pull back for a moment. Giving her a moment to regain her breath, he removed her clothing, pulling the gown, the stays, and finally the chemise over her head, and then tossing them aside, letting them land in a rustle of fabric somewhere far, far away from Rose's universe.

She reached out, finding and tugging impatiently at the clothing he still wore. "I want to feel all of you," she told him.

With a muttered oath, he ripped off the last articles of clothing, then lay against her, not trying to hide the hard length that pressed against her body. Rose pushed him away enough so she could move her hand down, and touch him there, curious how this most mysterious part of a man's anatomy actually felt.

Hard but smooth, warm, and heavy. She ran her fingers along the length of it, and traced the tip, earning a stifled, pleased groan from him.

"Well?" he asked after a moment.

"Interesting," she replied.

He laughed, sounding genuinely delighted. "You are unique, Rose."

"I would have to say the same of you," she said, still stroking him, intensely curious about how each little touch seemed to provoke a reaction in him. He must be very sensitive there, just as she was sensitive at her center, where his tongue teased that bud between the folds of her flesh. "So this will be inside me?"

"If you want. But not yet. There's much more to explore before that."

Rose was very happy to explore. She ran her hands all over him, and squeezed and stroked and licked wherever he seemed to have the strongest reaction. In turn, he kissed her newly naked breasts, and sucked on them until she panted and cried out that it felt too good to endure, and then he moved so that he could settle on top of her, her legs spread wide and her arms clinging to his shoulders.

"Ready, Rose?"

She nodded, not trusting herself to speak.

"I'm sorry that it will probably hurt a little," he told her, bending his head to give her a soft kiss on her mouth. He tasted like salt and smelled like sex, with faint lavender from the sheets sweetening the air.

Rose sucked in a breath, her body tensing up, her legs tight against his as he pushed into her. He was going slowly, so slowly, but she was also certain that something was wrong. It was too tight, too hot. She began to feel as though she would faint.

"*Breathe*, Rose," he ordered harshly.

She exhaled with a whoosh, not realizing she'd been holding her breath.

At the same time her body relaxed a little and he thrust once more.

Rose gasped in mixed pain and astonishment. Then the heat began, a slow pulse of delightful warm throbbing in her lower belly as he moved within her.

Each slight push and pull brought a wave of entirely new sensations, and all Rose could do was cling to Adrian as she reveled in the miracle of feeling him inside her own body. The pain faded as the pleasure built up layer upon layer. Rose kept whispering "Yes oh yes, yes oh yes," even as tears filled her eyes. She arched her back when he slid one hand under her bottom, lifting her to meet him.

She never wanted to be anywhere else. Only here, crying with joy as this man filled her whole world with intense pleasure, opening her mind to an ocean of feeling she didn't know was even there before.

In the midst of this, he pulled away from her without warning, withdrawing just as he groaned and collapsed next to her, his flesh slick with sweat, his breath coming fast as he uttered something into his pillow.

"Adrian?" she asked, concerned.

"One moment," he muttered, taking a ragged breath. "I nearly lost myself, that's all."

She whispered, "Is that how it's supposed to be? This...tingly feeling, like you can't ever be still again?"

"That's because I've not finished with you yet," he told her, sounding more like himself. Then he slipped his hand down and touched her as he had before, his fingers delving into the slick warmth of her body.

Rose cried out when he stroked her in a particular way and he seized on her reaction, repeating the move relentlessly, working her into a near frenzy of insane need and incoherent demands for more until she hit a threshold and crossed it, her body suddenly stiff, then loose and soft and spent.

Waves of bliss rolled over her, starting between her legs but not stopping there. Rose drifted for a moment, not even sure what happened or where she was, only knowing that she was happy.

After a long moment, Adrian slowly removed his hand, then lay next to her. "There. That should take care of, as you call it, the tingly feeling." He kissed her, his lips curved with amusement.

"Oh, my God, when can we do this again?" she asked, wiping the tears from her eyes.

He made a sound that was half moan, half laughter. "You're telling me you liked it."

"I loved it. It's the most wonderful thing I've ever felt in my life. Being so close to someone, feeling you actually inside me, touching. I want to kiss you more," she added impulsively.

"Fine idea." He lowered his mouth to hers, and Rose ran her tongue over his lips, eager and grateful and filled with joy. "You made me feel so wonderful, Adrian. I'll never forget this."

He slipped his arms around her waist and held her to him. "You say that like you're sailing on the next tide. We have all the time in the world, darling."

"We don't even have till dawn."

"There will be other nights."

"We don't know that. You can't know that."

Rose nuzzled her face between his neck and shoulder, wishing that she could just stay like this always, entwined and contented with him. He kissed her softly, his hands gently stroking her back as she drifted into sleep.

For hours, Rose moved half in and out of dreams, all of them hazy and sweet. She was aware of Adrian's presence next to her, and his scent, and the sound of him breathing, slow and steady. Sometimes his mouth moved against hers, and she once sucked on his fingers until his breathing became labored and he grew stiff with desire.

So, another joining, this time with Rose straddled over him, riding slowly as she learned a new set of sensations that brought her gasping to completion, falling over him as their mingled breathing returned to normal.

Her dreams would never be the same.

But night could not last forever, and at some point, Adrian woke her from a deep slumber to give her the unwelcome news that he had to take her home.

"And soon, love. Dawn's on the way, and you must return before anyone is awake to see you. Can you do that? Sneak back into your house and pretend you were there all night?"

"Yes, of course. I know my own house."

"I'd keep you here if I could," he said then.

"Too long and you'll regret it," she pointed out, for even a nobleman could not avoid the consequences of being caught with a young lady like Rose.

"I don't think I would. And you will soon learn this house."

Rosalind shook her head. "It's not so simple. You don't understand how different it feels. I should blindfold you for a day, and see how you like it!"

He stroked her wrist with his thumb. "If you were the woman to blindfold me, I would raise no objections at all."

"Adrian!" Rose was both scandalized and intrigued. The thought of teaching him how to feel the way she felt...that was an idea that made her blood race.

He laughed softly, his breath warm against her neck. "I'm open to new experiences, darling. Whenever you wish to teach me."

Rosalind was having trouble breathing normally. "I doubt there's anything I could teach you."

"That's where you are wrong," he promised. "Rose, we've a whole lifetime together."

"Excuse me?" she asked, certain she'd misheard.

"We're going to marry, Rose. I mean, if you accept my offer."

"Oh, Adrian...I don't need you to do that. I knew what I was doing when I accepted your invitation. I know it was only for a night."

"You thought I'd take you to bed for a *night*?" he asked, his tone incredulous. "And you honestly think that I'm going to just let you disappear after this? Rose, I want to marry you."

"You're very kind to offer, but Adrian, I'm not appropriate as a wife. We've talked about this before, have we not? I don't have the skills to be a housewife."

"Housewife? You'd be a viscountess!"

"Even worse. I definitely don't have the skills for that.

Unless viscountesses sing and play instruments all day."

"Well…they could. Not that the ones I'm familiar with have done so. But Rose, it doesn't matter. After this, you can't pretend as if nothing has happened."

"Why not?" Rose asked bluntly.

A long and puzzled silence followed.

"I will not tell. You will not tell. I'm never going to get married, so no one will ever know that I'm not a virgin. And you'll find a suitable bride from your class when you are ready to do so."

"I don't want a suitable bride, I want you."

She smiled and shook her head. "Perhaps we should talk about this later." Rose didn't want to think of mundane things, not after a night of illicit, sensuous pleasure. She'd never dreamed such a thing would happen to her, and she still didn't entirely believe it had. All she wanted was to treasure the feelings of bliss that swirled lazily within her.

"Later, then. But we will talk about it." Adrian gave Rosalind one last, lingering kiss, leaving her in a delighted haze. "It's getting close to morning. I'm heartbroken to tell you we have to leave this bed."

How did she dress? How did she get downstairs? How did she get into the carriage, and then across the city to her own home? Rose was too overwhelmed to notice any of these things. For her, the revelation of the previous night occupied all her thoughts.

The door of the carriage opened, and Adrian helped her out. "We're here," he told her in a low voice. "You're standing at the head of the straight path from the mews to the back door of your house."

"That goes to kitchens. It's never locked," Rose told him. "I'll be all right."

"Rose," he said then. "We're going to be together

again. I promise."

"I don't need promises, Adrian."

"I'm making one anyway. Give me a day or two, please?"

She smiled, knowing that he was watching her. "I'm not fleeing the country, you know."

"You'd better not. Now best get moving, love." He kissed her hand, his lips warm and challenging against her skin, sparking a reaction in her body. Then he released her and moved away so she could slip into the house without being noticed. Behind her, the sky began to blush, but she couldn't see it.

Chapter 18

Adrian spent the day in a haze. Rose destroyed him last night. She was a lover without inhibitions and with infinite curiosity. He was not ever going to sleep with another woman. He couldn't. It would be a total disappointment.

With Rose, he felt like he mattered, as if she wanted to not just make love to him but actually understand his own mind during the act of loving. She responded to everything with joy and affection and openness and the result was that he was ruined for the rest of his life.

He had to have her, just as he'd told Carlos before. Last night only confirmed his beliefs. He was going to marry Rose, give her his name, give her a home, and family and everything she wanted. Because he couldn't face the alternative, which was an existence without her.

So the next day, Adrian arrived at the Blake house at three. He knew the women were out, since the stableboy was very informative after receiving a few coins. Their absence was actually a good thing.

"Good morning, Alice," he greeted the maid who he had seen there before.

She tried to look cold, but failed. "Miss Blake is not at home, sir. I am sorry."

"Don't be. It's Mr. Blake I've come to call on."

"Oh!" Alice said, flustered. "I'll...I'll see if he's at home, sir. Do you mind waiting in the hall a moment?" She hurried away. Obviously, her instructions regarding him and other gentlemen had only covered keeping him away from Rosalind. Now she had to find out if the master would be "at home" to Adrian.

He did not wait long for the maid to reappear, hurrying down the corridor. "This way, sir." Alice led him not to the drawing room, but to a smaller study. Blake was enthroned there, seated at a desk piled high with law books and papers.

"Lord Norbury," he said, unsmiling. "Won't you sit down." It was not a request.

Adrian sat in a leather chair opposite the desk. "Am I disturbing you at your work, sir?"

"No matter. This conversation would have to happen at some point."

"You expected me?"

"I trust you have come to apologize."

Adrian raised an eyebrow. "For what? I thought I made it clear that I don't regret a thing I've done...toward Miss Blake, that is. The rest of my life would require more explanation, but you're not a priest, and I'm not looking for absolution."

"I don't doubt it," Blake noted sourly. "So you haven't come to apologize?"

"No."

"Then why have you come?"

"For your permission to ask for Miss Blake's hand."

"What?" Blake was beyond astonished. "Rosalind?"

"She's the only daughter you have, correct? Of course I mean Rosalind."

"You want to marry Rosalind."

Adrian wondered if he should have waited to have this conversation until later in the day. The man seemed a bit befuddled. "Yes, sir. I wish to marry Rosalind. And you are her father and guardian, are you not? Have I your permission to ask Rose for her hand?"

Mr. Blake responded with perfect, icy clarity, "No."

"Excuse me?" Adrian was taken aback. "I am the seventh Viscount Norbury. It's not as if I'm some unknown off the street. And I can certainly provide for her. I explained to you before that I enjoy her company."

"Based on half a dance and a carriage ride, and a musical performance? Absurd!"

"Well, in fact…" Adrian shrugged slightly, ready to admit that their acquaintance was not solely limited to that. Not that he wanted to play the "I've compromised your daughter" card. He much preferred to simply ask and be accepted because he would be a good match for her.

Blake did not let him continue. "I don't even want to know what other exchanges you might have had with her! Not to mention the gifts to the house. Have there been letters as well?"

"Only a few."

"I'll burn the ones in her possession."

Adrian was getting angry. "Let me remind you, Blake, I am discussing marriage here. Last time I checked, that wasn't scandalous. Rather the opposite."

"You honestly expect me to believe that you could make her happy?"

Adrian stared at him. "What does that mean?"

"A man of your reputation wouldn't know the first thing about a partnership like marriage. I know all too well what you think of women, your lordship. You might be amused by marriage for a few weeks, but you're a libertine through and through. You'd never remain faithful to

Rosalind, and you'd destroy her happiness when she learned about your deeds. And then where would she be? Blind, without her own family, and trapped in a loveless contract with a man who has no respect for society. What kind of guardian would I be if I allowed that?" Mr. Blake leaned back then, his brow sweating.

Adrian tried to keep hold of his emotions. "I think you have not heard me out, sir," he began quietly. "Yes, I have a reputation. But those deeds are in the past."

"I have heard of those past deeds. Reprehensible."

"I was younger then, I have changed. I truly care for Rosalind...I mean, Miss Blake."

Blake only shook his head. "No. It is not past. A duel just last month, over an affair with a man's wife. Tindell, wasn't it? I've been hearing things about you, Norbury. Recently. And what about an incident at Vauxhall Gardens this week?" He stared hard at Adrian, who blinked in surprise.

"What did you hear?"

Mr. Blake nodded grimly, convinced of Adrian's guilt. "I heard enough. You were there. So was Rosalind. I hoped it was not true, but I can tell you haven't changed."

"You mustn't blame her for any rumor you might have heard."

"I don't. She is innocent, led down a dark path by you for your own amusement."

"That is not true." Well, the path at Vauxhall had been dark. He doubted Blake would appreciate the joke.

"Maybe one day you will change. Maybe another man would trust you with his daughter. But not me. I've heard too much. Good day, sir." Blake deliberately opened a book and began to read it.

Adrian stood, furious. He had expected an argument, but not a complete refusal to even hear his side of the story. And who had Blake been hearing all this from? It had been a while since Adrian had done anything to bolster his shady reputation (at least, anything that was generally known to society). He wanted another chance to convince Blake, one that did not hinge on the fact that he'd already technically ruined Rose. Not that it felt like ruin. "Have you spoken to Rosalind about this?"

"Certainly not. And I will not. The faster she forgets about you, the better."

"How nice of you to make up her mind for her."

"That will do, my lord," Blake snapped. "You are in my house! I will run it, and my family, as I see fit."

Adrian walked to the door, but he turned at the threshold. "I understand your position, sir," he said quietly. "I see there's nothing I can do to convince you that you're wrong. But I want you to know that since I met Miss Blake, I've only ever wanted to ensure her happiness."

A strange expression crossed Blake's face, but he only said, "Good day, Lord Norbury."

Adrian left without another word.

When Adrian returned to his own house, Carlos was waiting with a bottle of champagne, which turned out to be wasted.

"He said no," Adrian reported dully, though underneath he was seething.

"No?"

"Correct. The opposite of the answer I was hoping for."

"Well, can't you just ask Rosalind directly and let her persuade her father? After all, he's not likely to ignore the wishes of his only daughter."

"I didn't think he'd be likely to ignore the proposal of a viscount, but here we are."

Carlos frowned. "Aren't you friendly with Prinny?

Ask him to intervene."

"This is *not* the sort of thing one bothers a monarch about," Adrian returned, appalled at the very notion. "First, he'd expect me to handle it on my own, and second, he's got bigger concerns than whether I'm getting married to the right girl."

"You went shooting together last fall, and he can do nothing?"

"He can do what he likes, but I'm not going to waste his time with this! I need to save a favor to ask him not to behead you when you inevitably *do* get caught by the law."

"I'm touched," Carlos said. "What were Blake's reasons for denying you?"

Adrian shrugged. "He thinks I'm a terrible person."

"Really? Just because of a lifetime of licentious behavior, dozens of duels, and your utter contempt for rules?"

Adrian didn't laugh at Carlos's sarcasm. "I need to prove that I'm not what he thinks I am."

Chapter 19

A FEW DAYS LATER, ROSE and Poppy were in the back garden of the Blake house once again. Rose had not breathed a word of what happened when Adrian took her to his house for the night. In the heat of the day, she was not entirely sure that it did happen…only to recall some particularly shocking and sensual memory that she was incapable of making up.

But she was happy. No, more than happy. She had done something for the sole reason of wanting to do it, and she didn't regret it for a moment. Adrian had said he'd find a way for them to be together again, and Rose trusted him, though she couldn't imagine what plans he was making. He told her it might take a few days, and she should be patient.

Well, patience was difficult, but she did her best.

Meanwhile, Poppy was reading to herself, grumbling over the latest selection. "Ugh, the early versions of 'Sleeping Beauty' are horrible! She's in the castle and this prince comes, but he doesn't rescue her, he just beds her —while she's sleeping!—and he gets her with child and she only wakes up after giving birth and her babies cry so much she can't sleep anymore…which is probably the most realistic part of the tale."

"Does a different prince rescue her?" Rose asked, only half listening, lost in reminiscing.

"No, the same one comes back and takes her home, but his mother is an ogre. Not as a euphemism. She's a literal ogre and she eats the babies."

"You're making things up, I've never heard that in 'Sleeping Beauty'!"

Poppy slapped closed the cover of the book she was holding. "I'm reading the original version, which is in French. They didn't make *that* version for the nursery."

Alice came out to the garden. "Excuse me. Letter for Miss Rose."

Poppy took it and said, "It's from Heather."

Rose hid her disappointment, hoping for word from Adrian. "She wrote us only a couple days ago, and Heather's not the most diligent correspondent. What's she say?"

Poppy read aloud:

Dear Rose,

It is imperative that we meet in person, for I have news that I dare not put to paper, and it cannot wait. Thanks to some business on Uncle's part, I shall be in London on Thursday. I'll call on you as soon as I am able. Will you stay home to meet me?

Heather

"It is Thursday!" Poppy said then. "Heather must have written just before she got in the coach."

Rose took a breath, disturbed at Heather's tone, so different from her usual breeziness. "What dire thing can have happened?" she asked Poppy. Rose remembered Heather's antics from their schooldays. She was bold and fearless from the first, so whatever occurred must be terrible indeed. "I wonder if she needs our help?"

"I can't imagine," said Poppy. "This is very odd. Well,

we were supposed to call on Lady Sara and a few others, but I suppose it can be put off. Perhaps it's good that Aunt Gertrude is at her church function all day."

"Indeed," Rose said. Her mother was a good person, but not exactly a beacon of calm in a storm.

"It's only addressed to you," Poppy mused. "I wonder why."

"She must have been in a state when she wrote it," Rose guessed. "She knows you are the one who reads me my letters anyway."

The girls waited anxiously as the hours ticked by. A few callers came, but not Heather. Then at four o'clock, Alice breathlessly announced Heather had arrived.

"For pity's sake, send her out here!" Rose ordered.

Heather came out onto the terrace and moved to greet them both. "I have only a short time, as we've got to return home later today. Uncle Fitz's been insistent that we not stay in London a moment longer than necessary."

"How are you getting on with him?" Rose asked, knowing that Heather had clashed with him in the past few months.

"Oh, it's up and down, depending on how much he's been drinking. Some days I hate him, and other days I remember that he's Papa's brother and he's doing his best, or at least what he thinks is the best."

Then Heather embracing them tightly, first Poppy, and then Rose, who she held longer.

"Oh, my dear," Heather breathed. "I am so sorry."

"Don't be sorry!" Rose told her. "Of course we want to hear what has happened to you. We'll do anything we can to help, of course."

Heather pulled away, startled. "Happened to me? Oh, sweethearts, no! It's what's happening to *you*, Rose."

"What?"

"You'd better tell us everything," Poppy added in a low voice. "Let's sit. I have a hunch we'll need to when we hear."

"It's terrible and so nasty, I can barely put it into words. But I swear it's true. I overheard Uncle Fitz and his cronies talking about it during their card game. They were laughing about it, and they didn't know I was there, so they had no reason to make up a tale just to shock me."

"What is it, for pity's sake?" Poppy demanded.

"You know that there's a habit among some gentlemen to cast wagers on wild things. Absurd happenings or silly bets, but also things…they try to create. Such as making a fool of a certain lady."

"Like that man leaving Rose on the dance floor," Poppy said. "I guess it's something like that."

"This is worse, but I think it may stem from the first event. One of my uncle's friends is just the type of man who will search out the strangest wagers on the books in the worst gaming hells and place money on them, just for the thrill of it. He placed a bet on you, Rose."

"*Me?*" Rose asked in confusion. "How? What does that even mean?"

"Oh, God forgive me for being the one to tell you." Heather inhaled, steeling herself. "There's a pool for the question of what date Rosalind Blake, the blind girl, will be seduced and ruined, as defined by being unmarriageable. Any man can bet, but there's higher stakes for the ones who bet on *themselves* doing the ruining. Apparently, one of the men who frequents that particular hell is none other than Viscount Norbury."

Rose's throat closed, and she sagged backward as her heart thudded ominously in her chest. Was this what happened when one died?

Poppy took her by the shoulders, holding her steady.

"Rose, Rose, listen. There must be more to this. Or Heather misheard! Or something."

"It's worse," Heather said. "Years ago, according to my uncle—who'd know because he wagered on the outcome like it was a horse race—there was a similar bet to ruin a young lady in Windsor. She *was* ruined, utterly, and finally left the country because she was so humiliated. The winner of that bet was a man named Adrian Marsh."

"Who later became Viscount Norbury," Poppy nearly spat out.

"Oh, no," Rose moaned. To think she'd been so foolish. He talked about marriage afterward, as if he truly… cared.

Poppy and Heather sat on either side of her, forming a shield between her and the world. Poppy said, "Rose, darling, speak to us."

"It all makes sense," she said miserably. "I was ignored by society, and then Norbury danced with me, and then I was surrounded by men all trying to get me alone. And Norbury was one of them, and…he *did* get me alone."

"He did?" Heather gasped.

Poppy squeezed her arm. "Tell me."

"The night you stayed with your parents, Poppy, and Mama was gone, and Lady Sara chaperoned me at the party…well, I left the party, but I ended up at Adrian's house. It wasn't my personal charm that made him want to seduce me," Rose said slowly. "It was some vile *wager*." How was that possible, when he asked her to sing, when he told her any number of times, even right to the end, that he would take her home if she said?

"Oh. My. God," Heather said heavily, her shoes stomping the ground as she cursed under her breath.

"You didn't say a word!" Poppy almost wept.

"What was I to say? I wanted to be there, and it was a…secret." Rose gasped in air, the memories of that night washing over her. Was she so easily manipulated?

"What are we going to do?" whispered Heather. "We have to do something to protect Rose from all this scandal!"

Rose's hands were all wet, and that was when she discovered she was crying.

Heather wrapped her in a hug, and dabbed at her face with a handkerchief, murmuring useless platitudes that nevertheless felt like very necessary advice. Rose could barely think at the moment, and what if her friends weren't with her now? It didn't bear thinking about.

"Then why is this bet still on?" Poppy asked, to no one in particular. "If all he wanted was to ruin you, he'd have told the world about it and collected his winnings. But he hasn't."

"Perhaps he gets more money if he waits till a certain day," Heather guessed.

"He did tell me it might take him a few days before he…" Rose choked up for a moment. "Lord, I'm such a fool."

Poppy's silence indicated that Heather's guess could be correct. But then she said, "Listen, I'll speak to his friend. I'll get Mr. de la Guerra to tell me what's going on."

"And you'd trust him to tell you the truth?" Heather demanded. "He's probably part of the whole plan!"

"If he is, I'll scare him away from England forever," Poppy said grimly.

Chapter 20

CARLOS STORMED INTO THE ROOM, disturbing Adrian's quiet reading.

"What the hell?" Adrian asked crossly.

Carlos handed him a newspaper, pointing to a particular column. Adrian took it gingerly, disliking the feel of the grimy ink on his fingers. Then he saw that the article in question was a poem, by Anonymous, titled "The Rose Deflowered."

Sweet Rose stripped of beauty, petals plucked one by one,

Shame on all! Will we not see what the rogue has done?

Denuding English gardens, a thief in the night,

With only ruined blossoms left in dawn's pale light...

He stopped reading, his heart going cold. He'd been so careful! There was no way anyone would have seen Rose and him together that night.

"This is clearly about Rosalind Blake," Carlos said. "And you're the rogue."

"It's rubbish. No one was ever convicted by poetry."

"This isn't a court of law, Adrian! This is London society, and a few hints are all that's needed to condemn a person."

"Has anyone said her name? Or mine?"

"Not that I know of...at least, not openly. Just some heavy hints that you're involved somehow, mostly because everyone knows you've befriended the family. But there are rumors flying that Miss Blake is, ah, open for business."

Adrian stood up. "I better have heard that wrong."

"*I'm* not saying it, you idiot. Other people are. It's just a low rumble now, in the clubs and the various hells. It has not yet, to my knowledge, passed to the women's gossip circles, probably because there's no proof to bolster it. But any scrap of evidence, not matter how flimsy, could make the rumors stick. And if the ladies of London decide that the rumor has teeth, your friend is done for in any social circle of note. And you know, there's the...past bet." Carlos added that last part softly, as if that would make it less real.

"God damn it, I'm never going to escape my youth, am I? Then I've got to make sure no one fans the flames."

"Are you really the best person to do this?" Carlos asked. "I mean, you're hardly known as a guardian of ladies' virtue."

"It was the ladies who made that choice, not me," Adrian said. "After my mistake, I've never ruined virgins."

"Until you met Rosalind." Carlos paused, looking askance. "*Did* you ruin her?"

"In what sense?" he hedged. After all, a woman was only ruined if people knew about it.

"Oh, Christ." Carlos closed his eyes and walked toward the window, away from Adrian. "All right, this is messy."

"It's not your mess," Adrian replied, rather bitterly.

"You can jaunt off to start another revolution, if you like. After all, it's been what, six months since the last time you attempted to bring down a government?"

"That last time was barely a revolution," Carlos said, momentarily distracted. "More of a demonstration of force. We got the attention of the powers that be. And this conversation is not about that, Adrian! It's about your little English rose."

Just then a footman entered and held a tray out to Carlos. "Came this afternoon, sir," he explained.

Carlos accepted the letter, and opened it quickly. "It's from Poppy," he said, scanning it intently. "Oh, no. They've heard. A friend learned of it and told both Rosalind and Poppy. Damn it. It would have been better if they didn't know."

"I'll go there immediately," Adrian said, standing. "I need to see Rose and explain things. She'll be upset."

"No, wait. Let me read." Carlos looked up. "Poppy wants to speak to me, to get an explanation. She says that Rose is devastated, and refuses to see anyone at all, including you. No one will be admitted to call upon either girl."

"Then how will you meet Miss St. George?"

"Her stepfather's warehouse," Carlos said, glancing at the clock. "I'm to be there at six. That doesn't leave much time."

He left as quickly as he arrived, and Adrian sat alone, glaring into the low flames of the fireplace.

Not long after, the footman returned with another newspaper, a coffeepot, and a letter from Adrian's mother.

Adrian ignored the paper and opened the letter; it was as if the dowager were in the room with him, offering a tirade of opinion whether he wanted it or not. There were rumors as far as Bath that Lord Norbury was dallying with a very innocent, virginal young lady who he obviously had no intention of marrying. Adrian was besmirching the family name. He was making a mockery of some of the most vaunted social institutions that perpetuated the very order of things. He had not written to his mother frequently enough. The dowager viscountess was left with no choice.

She was returning to London to take matters into her own hands.

"God help me," Adrian muttered. What a mess if his *mother* decided to meddle in things now.

* * * *

"Mr. de la Guerra," Poppy said coldly.

She had been waiting for him in the small office adjacent to the warehouse. People were working there, but Poppy was alone in the room. The fury radiated off her in freezing waves. Carlos once fell overboard in the North Atlantic, swimming though frigid waters in a desperate attempt to reach a rope and haul himself to safety, shivering on deck and nearly dying of exposure.

This was worse.

"I didn't know what was happening, I promise," he said. "I mean, I knew about some wagers, but not about Adrian sneaking off to see Rosalind..."

"And why should I believe you?"

He shrugged helplessly. "I don't know. There's no reason you ought to, I suppose. But I assure you that Adrian never gambled a penny on Rose."

"There was a poem in a paper today," she said. "A *poem*! It practically accused Rose of acting like a...like a..." Poppy's normal confidence deserted her, and she inhaled sharply to prevent a flood of tears.

Carlos stepped up to her, putting one hand on her shoulder. "I saw the poem. I showed Norbury, and he's going to handle it. We're not going to let anyone get away with this."

She shrugged away from him. "Excuse me, but someone already has! Rose is ruined now, and she's got no chance of a proper marriage. Who's going to offer for her after this scandal?"

"Norbury will."

Poppy stared at him in astonishment, which quickly turned to rage. "Oh, so he's finally caught, is he? London's most prolific rake is somehow going to realize the error of his ways now and marry a woman who brings a modest dowry and no title or lands with her? Do you not realize how marriages work here in England?"

Carlos shot back, "I realize that Norbury cares about Miss Blake. She won't face this situation alone."

"She's not alone! She has her parents, and she has her friends, and she has *me*." Poppy's eyes went bright. "Norbury played with her affections, and he's not going to get a chance to ride in and play knight in shining armor now. *He's* the reason she's locked herself in the bedroom and hasn't eaten anything all day."

"Norbury can speak to her, reassure her—"

"What is his word worth?" Poppy snapped. "This was the same man who placed the same bet years ago, and guess what? A woman was ruined then. Why should we believe that the outcome will be different this time? You can just tell him that he's not welcome at the Blake house anymore. Mr. Blake has made it known that he'll never cross the threshold again. Thank God we're going to leave the city! I just pray Rose will recover in time…"

"Where? When are you going?"

"We don't know yet, and that's not your concern! All I

wanted to say today is that Norbury should be ashamed of what's he done."

"Perhaps that's what you think…"

"That's what *Rose* thinks. She never wants to speak to Norbury again, and I'm here to tell you that. The game is over, Mr. de la Guerra. Call in the wager, collect the winnings, whatever it is you *gentlemen* do." Poppy shook her head once, adding in a low voice, "I thought you were different."

She turned away, then pointed to the warehouse door. "Go. Leave here, and then leave London, and then leave England altogether on your stupid boat, or in a much smaller wooden container for all I care! I hope I never see you again!"

* * * *

A few hours after he left, Carlos returned to Adrian's house, his normally cheerful expression now grave. He smelled like he'd stopped by a tavern or four on his way back.

"What did she say?" Adrian asked.

"It did not go well," Carlos growled. "They think you were merely toying with Rosalind's affections. I tried to persuade Poppy that you have nothing to do with any wagers, but she is utterly convinced that you are merely continuing a lifetime of roguish behavior and you are not serious about Rose at all."

"What? I told her father I want to marry her."

"From her reaction, he never told anyone of that conversation."

"I told *Rose* I want to marry her. Or I implied it." Had he? He'd been distracted.

"It seems she did not think the offer was sincere…

perhaps because you mentioned it at the wrong moment."

His friend was being unusually tactful about all this, Adrian had to admit. Carlos could have said that Adrian was an idiot for only bringing up marriage when they were in bed together after he'd thoroughly compromised her.

"Look, I'll write a letter to Rose, with the offer of marriage stated so it's clear. I'll deliver it personally—"

"You won't get past the front door, and I suspect that any letter would be burned rather than read. Mr. Blake has apparently declared us *personae non grata*, and Rose has locked herself in her room."

"Then you can appeal to Poppy to slip the letter to her."

"No I can't! Miss Poppy suggested that I leave England at the earliest possible moment, hopefully in a coffin. As rejections go, hers was the most definitive I've ever gotten."

Adrian looked up, catching something in Carlos's tone. "You like her, don't you?"

"She was intriguing," Carlos said, obviously attempting for nonchalance. "But the world is filled with women. Anyway, she's not my type."

Oh, his friend had fallen hard. Adrian knew how it felt, and he hated that he'd ruined not just his own relationship, but another one as well. "What did she say, exactly?"

"She said she thought I was different," Carlos replied quietly.

There wasn't much passion in the words, but Adrian could tell that Poppy's judgment had crushed his friend, more than anything else she might have said.

"I will fix this," Adrian promised. "All of it."

"How are you going to do that when we're not even

allowed to speak to anyone in the Blake household?"

Before Carlos could respond, the unmistakable sound of wheels on gravel made them both go still.

Then Adrian jumped up, moving to the window overlooking the front.

This was a nightmare, wasn't it?

No. It was all too real.

The dowager viscountess was alighting from the coach, her expression hinting of the storm to come.

"I thought your mother went to Bath," Carlos said, joining him at the window.

"She did, but now she's back, because I've made such a mess that she's heard of it even that far away. God help me."

* * * *

Early the next day, the dowager viscountess summoned Adrian to her sitting room, where she sat in a high, wing-backed chair by the fireplace, which was burning despite it being a fine spring morning. She wore a pale yellow dressing gown adorned with yards of Belgian lace, and a similarly lacy cap covered her hair (but framed her pinched mouth and hard eyes). The total effect was something like being brought into the presence of an extremely angry, sentient iced pastry.

"Adrian, I am not pleased," she announced, quite unnecessarily.

"You're not alone."

"You will give me an account of your doings since I left, unvarnished and honest. Leave nothing out."

He moved to sit in the chair opposite hers, but she gestured for him to stand, right in front of the fireplace. He felt like a schoolboy forced to recite his Latin lessons while standing in the flames of hell. Eton had never been this bad.

"At Lady Herbert's party, just before you left for Bath, I happened to meet a young lady named Rosalind Blake."

"I have never heard of her. Who are her people?"

Adrian sighed inwardly. Here came the judgment. "In terms of titles, no one of consequence. Her father is a barrister, quite well-respected, I've come to discover."

"And what dowry?"

"Very little. I think they never expected her to marry."

"Why ever not? She cannot be hideous or without charm, or you would not have noticed her."

"She's blind."

"Blind?" his mother echoed. "She cannot see?"

"That's the general definition of the word, yes."

"Don't be pert with me, young man. What was a blind girl doing at Lady Herbert's party in the first place?"

"Dancing." Adrian explained the situation, and how Rose's partner had abandoned her on the floor, leading Adrian to swoop in to finish the dance so no one noticed and the lady wouldn't be embarrassed by the attempted trick.

"I didn't realize she was blind until we were actually dancing, and then it became quite obvious that the intention had been to create a scene with her at the center, lost amid all the moving people."

His mother sniffed in disdain. "Some men should not be allowed among society. But that was well done of you, Adrian, to mitigate the damage."

"I fear it just caused more trouble. After the dance, I escorted Rose—Miss Blake—out to the garden." He hastened to give his reasons and explained the kiss, and Rose's effect on him with her clever responses and unexpected candor. He told about going to meet her and running into her in the park, how he couldn't remember ever having as much *fun* with a person since he was young. How her singing enchanted him. How one encounter become more, and how he realized that he needed her in his life. How she was not just pretty, but intelligent—

"Enough!" His mother held up one hand. "Clearly you fell in love with this woman. *Do* you love her? Not just affection or lust, but love?"

The way her eyes bored into his left no room for dissembling. Adrian nodded. "Yes, I love her. I want to spend the rest of my life with her."

She nodded back. "Then that's that. Not the match I'd been expecting perhaps, but what's done is done. What confuses me is that if you've been courting her and there is even a suggestion that it is serious, why you have not already proposed to her?"

"I did. Well, I intended to ask her father for permission. But by the time I was able to ask, he refused my suit."

The dowager viscountess (a woman who could count her ancestors back to the Conqueror) gasped in disbelief. "He *what*?"

"Mr. Blake was acquainted with my past, including the various…associations…I've had…"

"Just say affairs. Let us speak plainly."

"My affairs, then. He felt that I could not make Rose happy."

"He does not believe that you are good enough for her?" she asked, her tone rising as she spoke.

"In short, yes. I tried to argue my case, but, well, he's the barrister. And the judge, apparently. I left the house after being told that not only would Rose never be allowed to marry me, I was not to see her ever again."

"This is ludicrous. You are the Viscount Norbury!"

"That's what I said. He was unmoved."

"I will move him." She pushed on the arms of her chair to propel her to her feet. "I am issuing an invitation to the Blake family for tea. They will come, and we will talk, and all will be resolved. You will be engaged before dessert, and this scandal will die the quick death it deserves."

As plans went, it had the virtue of simplicity. An invitation from the dowager viscountess held the weight of social approval, and to refuse it would be unthinkable. Adrian never expected his mother to throw herself into the problem in such a direct way, but he felt a swell of gratitude that she had, even without meeting Rose herself. It didn't matter that society valued Rose less because she was blind, or didn't have the luck to be born into the aristocracy. His mother trusted his judgment. Which, after the many mistakes he'd made in younger years, meant the world to him.

Chapter 21

ROSE HAD NOT LEFT HER room since learning the truth about Adrian. She didn't want any food, so it was easy to skip meals. She half-heartedly opened one of the few books she owned that were intended to be read by the blind, thanks to the invention of a writing style by a Frenchman named Charles Barbier a few years previously. Unfortunately, not many books were available in night writing or other tactile systems. And Rose had read all of hers many times, so nothing could hold her attention now.

Rose curled under the covers of her bed, praying for sleep yet resigned to wakefulness. What she hadn't told Poppy, or anyone, was that her mind constantly replayed every conversation with Adrian, every kiss, every touch. She could recall the night he made love to her with perfect clarity, and even now her body warmed at the memory of his hands and his mouth on her skin.

She was still in her night rail even though the clock had chimed noon. She was cradled in the familiar softness, the scent of the laundry soap that Alice used, and the purring of the kitten Ralph, curled up against her, his tiny body radiating warmth.

"Let's never leave the house again," she told the cat.

He meowed in agreement, apparently quite content

where he was.

Just then, the door squeaked open. "Rose, are you awake?" Poppy asked.

"Yes." She wished she were asleep, but alas.

"Your parents want you to come downstairs."

"Why?"

"I think they want to discuss something with you."

"Tell them I'm sleeping."

"They told me that if you were sleeping, I was to wake you up. I think it's important."

"Oh, fine. But the cats must come too." She heard the mewing of Miss Mist, who'd been sleeping on Poppy's bed earlier.

"Yes, let's bring them. Whatever is being discussed, cats will help, I'm sure."

In the parlor, Rose moved to the long chaise, where she sat down and then held out her hands for Ralph, who stopped squeaking in annoyance and immediately began to purr the moment he nestled against Rose's chest.

"What is it?" Rose asked dully.

"We've received an invitation to tea," her mother said.

"No." She did not want to have to sit and sip with anyone, not now. This was what was so important that she had to be dragged out of her room?

"Tea with Lady Norbury."

Rose gasped. How could that even be? For one, Adrian said his mother was in Bath, and second, even if she returned to London, why would the lady want to be associated with a ruined woman?

"It is for this afternoon," Mr. Blake added. "She seems impatient."

"Attempting to patch over the scandal somehow," Mrs. Blake said. "But I don't believe that any good can come of this. She must not know the details, and thinks this is easily solved."

"It is easily solved," Poppy pointed out. "Rose can marry Norbury."

"No, she cannot," Mr. Blake shot back. "No daughter of mine will be foisted off on an uncaring rogue. If he offered for you, Poppy, I'd say the same."

"Well, he hasn't, thank goodness. But if we do not allow Lady Norbury to bully us into...whatever she's thinking about, we still need to decide what to do about it."

"That can be discussed later," Mr. Blake said. His breath came heavily, and Rose worried that the strain of the scandal was hurting her family as much as her.

"Are you feeling all right, Papa?" she asked.

"What? Yes, never better, darling. Now listen. You girls are to remain here for the day. Your mother will respond to this invitation, and I will make some inquiries about what we may do about all this." He did not sound hopeful.

Mrs. Blake leaned over to give Rose a hug. "This must be terrible for you, dear, but no matter what, we are here to stand by you. Remember, nothing lasts forever."

"Yes, Mama," she responded, thinking that her mother had grown up almost as much as she had over the past decade. It was true, wasn't it. Nothing lasted forever... especially love.

Rose wished she'd never learned that lesson.

* * * *

Later that afternoon, Rose sat outside in the garden with Poppy. Alice brought out a letter, which Poppy opened immediately.

Dear Rose,

Heather has written to me in great haste and concern. She won't say why (on paper), but she begged me to take you both in for the summer. Not that begging is required— you are both welcome to my home at any time. However, I am pleased to tell you that my old home of Rutherford Grange is also available for your exclusive use, should you wish more privacy than Lyondale would provide. In fact, I shall direct that the Grange is prepared for your imminent arrival. And should you need anything else, simply ask. What is the point of being a duchess if one cannot aid one's friends?

Daisy

Poppy read the letter out loud, then fell silent, awaiting Rose's opinion.

Over the past few days, the spate of rumors and whispered gossip had taken its toll on Rose. It didn't matter that a number of the gentlemen who first suggested dalliances with her had all—rather suddenly—retracted their statements and loudly announced that of course they had nothing evil to imply about Miss Blake, who was an innocent, an angel, etc. etc. Their newly voiced defenses only served to bolster the underlying belief that something scandalous had occurred, and of course it was all Rose's fault.

She avoided speaking to anyone about it, despite the number of people calling at the house, who were doubtless eager to discuss it.

"Lady Sara is at the door," Alice said, coming up to the girls.

"We're not at home to anyone," Rose mumbled.

"I told her that already, and she insisted I bring up her card. She wrote something upon it." Alice left after Poppy took the card from the tray.

Poppy read aloud, "'Miss Blake ought to deny all rumors and leave for the country until autumn. This is the only way to quell the gossip.'"

Rose sighed. "I know she means well, but I suspect that every time anyone breathes a word about this, it makes it worse. If I deny it, they'll all say I have must *something* to deny, and therefore it is all real."

"Probably," Poppy agreed. "But there is something to be said for leaving London for a while. I'm glad Daisy has arranged for us to stay at Rutherford Grange. It is very secluded there, and you can enjoy some peace and quiet. Your parents will surely approve, and we can leave in the next few days."

Rose doubted that she'd enjoy much about her exile, even though she would be glad to spend time with Daisy, who'd be living nearby. She remembered Rutherford Grange as a pleasant place, surrounded by woods and fields, each with their own sounds and scents, so utterly different from the urban bustle of London's streets. Not to mention that Daisy, now married to a duke, could offer a degree of protection from harassment.

"It will be good to have a change," Rose said, trying to be agreeable. All she could think was that she'd be far, far away from Adrian. Shouldn't she want that? She hated him! And anyway, he was done with her, having got what he wanted. She hadn't heard a thing from him since... well, since she discovered the awful truth.

She knew that Poppy had spoken with Adrian's friend once, but Poppy had never told her anything useful out of that conversation. It was a pity, really. Rose could tell that Poppy had rather lost her heart to Mr. de la Guerra. But surely it would be difficult for them to spend any time together, after *his* best friend ruined *her* best friend.

It was, to say the least, an awkward situation.

Why did love have to be so painful? Such highs and lows, and she was not equipped to deal with either. Far better to live out her days as a lonely spinster, keeping her parents company into their old age. And perhaps she could someday be Auntie Rose to her friends' children, abiding in a spare room, making herself as useful as possible for a blind lady no one wanted…

"Are you moping?" Poppy broke into her thoughts. "You mustn't, dear. I promise everything will be fine, somehow. We may need to offer ourselves as brides to some men in far-flung parts of the world, but we'll manage. Did you know that some men accept brides fresh out of Bridewell prison? Next to them, we'll surely be sought after!"

Rose shook her head. "Don't joke. You'll find a good man to marry, just as your mother did…twice! I have resigned myself to whatever comes."

"Oh, Rose, don't you dare. There must be a way out of this mess."

With bitter irony, Rose retorted, "I can't see one."

Chapter 22

THE HOUR FOR TEA WAS getting close, so Adrian had his valet select a suitable outfit and dressed with special care. Though he'd already made his disastrous first impressions on the family, it might not be too late to make amends.

But when he went downstairs, his hands shaking at the thought of facing Mr. Blake again, the house was quiet.

He found his mother in the drawing room, but with no tea service in sight. Had he got the time wrong? (Adrian did not often participate in teas, which he regarded as boring and staid.)

"Well, shall we get ready for our guests?" he asked.

"No. The Blakes have sent their regrets. Prior obligations," his mother added in astonishment. "What could be more important?"

"Mr. Blake is involved in some very important case, I think. He may not have been able to get away."

"And Mrs. Blake? She's not arguing before the bar."

"She has many charitable commitments."

"What are you not telling me, Adrian? Why would the parents of a girl caught in an upsetting scandal not leap at any chance to end the problem?"

He would have to tell her everything. "It's more than upsetting, and there's a reason Rosalind Blake views me as worse than being alone."

"Go on."

So he told her. Told her about the stupidity of his youth, how he set so much store by the words and deeds of old schoolmates just out of Eton, young men who thought they knew everything just because they'd gotten a school-leaving certificate. How Adrian might technically be considered an adult but was really still a foolish boy. How he allowed himself to be drawn into the sort of mischief that was only "mischief" for privileged boys, but was destruction for anyone who got caught in the way. Like the young woman who his group of friends had decided to target—a shy girl living in Windsor, pretty and chaste and far too trusting.

Adrian had bet that he'd be the one who took her virginity, and he specified the date he'd do so, just to show off. It became a game, him against a few others, and for a few weeks, that girl had thought she was the most popular prize in Windsor...and she was, just not in the way she thought.

It hadn't been difficult to seduce her, and Adrian had almost convinced himself that it was harmless fun. He'd even managed to think that there would be no lasting consequences...until he did collect his winnings (using a letter from her that admitted the deed). Within a day, the word was out throughout the town, and though Adrian's name was bandied about (along with the other young men who'd bet), he never suffered a bit of censure. But he never saw her again, and he left the town shortly after, fleeing back home to the family estate, where no one knew what he'd done.

"She left Windsor. She left England, actually," Adrian finished his story. "It was worse than just a dalliance, because everyone knew she'd been ruined because of a wager. Not because someone wanted her so much he couldn't wait. Or any other version of the tale."

"The poor girl."

"She wasn't that poor afterward," he added. "We paid her off."

"We?"

He admitted, "I got the money from Father. I had to tell him what happened to get it."

"And he never breathed a word of it to me," she said.

"He didn't want you to know. He knew you'd be disappointed."

"What was the girl's name?"

"Alba. Her father worked for the college. He resigned his post after…" Adrian shook his head. "She never told her parents it was me, even with the rumors, she refused to give a name. She didn't want any connection. She just wanted to get away."

As he spoke, he couldn't shake how history was repeating itself, despite all his attempts to live his life differently.

"If she never told her father, how did he know who to press for payment?"

"He never did. Alba managed to get in contact with Carlos. Everyone in Windsor knew that we were friends, and even though I'd fled home after the scandal, Carlos stayed on. He was the go-between. And honestly, I'm rather surprised that he still kept me on as a comrade. He was furious with me."

"Perhaps he is a better friend than I'd given him credit for," she said grudgingly. "I always thought him to be a rabble-rouser."

"Oh, he is. But he's probably a lot smarter than I am, even if he never completed his studies."

"And now things have come full circle."

"But they shouldn't!" Adrian burst out. "That's what doesn't make sense. I *never* bet on Rose. I'd kill myself before ever doing that with any woman. But Blake must have heard about those past rumors, not to mention all the other accounts of affairs since then. And the duels. I'll own up to affairs and duels. But the betting…no."

"Yet that's what Mr. Blake is using as a reason to forbid a marriage. And I must say that any parent would take pause after hearing such a thing."

"Turns out my name and money and otherworldly magnetism isn't enough in the end," he concluded, his voice heavy with sarcasm. "I'll have to find some young lady who's mercenary enough to not care about any of it, so long as she gets her title and her pin money."

"So that is why you've never considered the opinion of your class since then. I wondered why you'd changed so much after finishing at Eton. Why you ignored all our advice to set yourself up for a society marriage and carry on the line. Why you went wild and mocked all the husbands and gentlemen by having affairs with their wives."

"I suppose so. I never thought of it like that."

"It seems quite obvious in retrospect. So the task that is set before you now is to convince the Blake family that you do love Rosalind, and are worthy of her."

But Adrian shook his head. "It's too late."

"What sort of son have I raised?" she asked, getting up from the table. She went out the door and left him alone to brood.

* * * *

He brooded for hours. Despite his words, he became convinced that there was something he could do to prove to Mr. Blake that he was worthy of Rosalind. Both Blake and Carlos had mentioned that many rumors and tales of Adrian's past had resurfaced recently. He doubted that was a coincidence. He had to find the source of these rumors and put a stop to them.

When he returned, Carlos had a few ideas of his own. "We need to find the author of that godawful poem. Maybe a past mistress or lover, looking to get back at you?"

Adrian shook his head. "Why wait so long? None of these rumors are new. And they're circulating among the wrong crowd. A woman's rumor mill operates through the salons and through her friends. You said Rose's friend heard them via men who were playing cards, which means they must have heard them at clubs."

"So a man, then," Carlos quickly revised his theory. "A husband."

"No. A husband with a grievance seeks out a duel," Adrian said. "He wants to defend his own name and honor, not tarnish mine further."

"Yes, but dueling with you rarely ends well for anyone else. Perhaps this man is too frightened to confront you directly, hence this stupid poem in the paper."

Adrian nodded. "That's a theory. But again, I haven't offended anyone in the past several months."

"Well, someone thinks differently," Carlos stated flatly.

The pair spent the evening visiting their own clubs, knowing that it would be difficult to get any man to speak of the rumors directly.

"Oh, rumors," said one acquaintance they'd finally found liquored up enough to talk freely. "They flare up now and then, don't they? But who believes them? I mean, I heard you seduced some virgin this week, spirited her right away from her chaperone at a ball or some such.

Wish I'd hear those whispers about my exploits," he added, grumbling.

Adrian was furious. It was one thing to hear his own ancient scandals thrown up against him, but it was chilling to hear this new and precise description, as if someone had specifically been following him. Worse, Rosalind was a victim too... He suddenly understood Mr. Blake's fear in a way he hadn't before. Rosalind's reputation, unlike his, couldn't withstand even a hint of impropriety. He had to find the source of these oddly detailed rumors to protect her, even if he never saw her again.

"Norbury?" Carlos asked, watching him. "What's the plan?"

"It hasn't changed," he said. "It's simply more urgent. I'll find who's responsible for these stories, and then I'll run a sword through him." Adrian turned on his heel and stalked out of the club.

"It has a certain direct charm," Carlos muttered, hurrying after his friend. In the street, he thought out loud. "The odd thing is, why bring Miss Blake into this at all? If someone wishes to harm your chances of courting her––perhaps he's a rival?––it would be counterproductive to hurt her reputation as well. I mean, unless there is someone in London who has equal cause to hate you both! And who do you both have in common? You and Miss Blake live in separate worlds."

Adrian stopped suddenly, staring at his friend.

"What?" Carlos asked.

"Someone we have in common. Someone who wants revenge for what he perceives as his embarrassment. Someone petty enough to hurt a woman he barely knows."

"I take it you have a candidate."

"I do," Adrian growled. "Now we just have to find

him."

It didn't take long. In a popular gaming hell, Adrian sighted a figure in a long black velvet jacket, standing near the dicing table. Carlos followed his gaze. "Jonathan Hynes? That no-account? You used to associate with him, didn't you?"

"Years ago. When I was less discriminating about the company I kept."

"Well, your choice of friends is better now, if I do say so myself. But he didn't wager on Miss Blake getting ruined."

"Yes, his name was conspicuously absent."

Adrian stalked up to the black-clad figure. Just as Hynes tossed the dice in his hands, Adrian said in a mild voice, "I should think you'd get sick of losing."

Hynes jumped at the words, but recovered quickly. He watched the dice turn up poorly and his stake removed from the table.

He laughed his loss off. "Ah, Lord Norbury. I didn't expect to see you here tonight. You seem to have shifted to musicales and knitting circles."

A number of men within earshot laughed at Hynes's comment. Then Carlos stepped behind Adrian, glaring at the circle in general, and the chuckles quickly died.

"The reason I've come, Hynes," Adrian said in a quiet voice, "is because there's something in this place that I simply can't find anywhere else."

"Excitement? Money? A sense of humor?" Hynes snapped, his eyes nevertheless betraying his nervousness.

"A liar." Adrian looked Hynes over deliberately.

"You are calling me a liar?"

"No. I'm calling you a petty, sniveling, cowardly liar who would spread false rumors about a blind woman simply because you couldn't make a fool of her at that party after you had bet your friends that you could." Adrian was guessing, but his instinct was good, and he knew Hynes's mind.

"Further, you sought to profit on a later wager made by a bookmaker, probably by suggesting the wager to him. Though you were careful not to bet yourself, you instructed a number of other men to do so, offering to cover their stakes. Which meant that every one of those men owed you. And you'll see to it that they pay at very high interest, won't you?"

Again, it was a guess. But from the hunted look in Hynes's eye, Adrian felt sure he was right.

This was news to the crowd, and several men frowned and began to mutter to their neighbors. It was one thing to destroy a young lady's life, but apparently far worse to offer poor terms on a loan.

Hynes blustered, saying, "This is all conjecture!"

"I've spoken to Evans, Lloyd, Atkinson, and Sir Richard. They'll confirm what I've said," Adrian told him in an icy tone. "And just to ensure that nothing unfortunate happens to them before they can talk, I've arranged for them to write their statements in front of a witness." He was improvising, and it felt good.

"You are quite mad."

"And, as I previously stated, you are a greedy, stupid coward." Adrian turned to Carlos. "That is what I previously stated, correct?"

"Close, but you could add *uncouth* and *bad dancer* and *repugnant to women*," Carlos noted. "Oh, and a dog could write a better poem than you can, Hynes."

"That's enough slander!" Hynes hissed. "I demand an apology!"

Adrian leaned back and smirked, summoning all his disdain for the other man and letting it show in his face.

"Absolutely not."

"Then you'll meet me at dawn!" Hynes declared.

Adrian felt a burst of triumph. "Excellent. I'll be there. Oh, and I choose swords."

"Swords?" Hynes echoed, suddenly realizing what he had committed to.

"Well, *you* insisted on the duel," Adrian said, not mentioning that he had very deliberately goaded Hynes into doing it. "I accepted, and it is my right to choose the weapon." Once a challenge was issued and accepted, the thing had to be seen through. Such were the rules of polite society.

"That is correct," Carlos noted in a detached tone. "I will serve as the viscount's second. Who will be yours?"

Hynes glanced around, eyes wild. His former friends had made a wide circle around him. None looked at him. He cast about for an ally. "Eberling! You'll do it!"

"I will?" a drunken man asked, looking rather chagrined to be singled out in this way.

"You'll be my second," Hynes insisted, looking as if he hoped the drunk would volunteer to fight first.

"Splendid," Carlos said, grinning. "Darthmore Abbey at dawn, in the field by the elms. I trust you know it. We'll even bring the surgeon. Good night, Hynes. I wish you pleasant dreams."

So Lord Norbury and Mr. de la Guerra stepped out of the gaming hell, breathing in the night air.

"Lot of things to take care of by dawn," Carlos said. "I'll locate a surgeon and do what else needs to be done. Why don't you go back to your house and relax for a few hours."

Adrian gripped him by the shoulder. "You're a true friend, Carlos."

"Are you going to kill him? Ridding London of a

snake like Hynes may be seen as an act of generosity."

"I don't kill."

"But this is a special situation, far more personal than anything else you've been pulled into. Miss Blake isn't one of those bored wives seeking an affair to liven up their existence. She's a young lady with very little experience, and what's more, you actually care for her."

"That's why I'm not going to kill him. I really don't want to propose to her over a corpse. Not that she'll be there, thank God."

"For someone who pretends to be such a rogue, you've got an annoyingly consistent moral code," Carlos said, but laughed as he did so, obviously rather proud of his friend.

"I've built it up over time," Adrian said. "No one noticed because they were busy talking about the scandals."

"Well, one way or another, you'll be noticed tomorrow."

"Do you think I'm doing the right thing?" he asked, suddenly unsure. Perhaps he was not thinking straight, too driven by his feelings for Rose rather than cold practicality.

"By defending Miss Blake's honor? By acting nobly, instead of scorning your birth and your family name? Adrian, you're *finally* doing the right thing."

"I hope she thinks so. I don't know how I'll explain it to her."

Carlos merely smiled. "Get some rest and leave everything to me. Just be ready to get in a carriage before dawn."

Chapter 23

VERY LATE THAT SAME NIGHT, Poppy was roused from her bed by the maid Alice, who was holding a candle.

"Miss, I'm so sorry. A boy just brought this letter round. He said it was a matter of life and death. He insisted I wake you. It's not my fault!"

Poppy blinked groggily. "A letter? Shouldn't you have woken Mr. Blake?"

"It's addressed to you." She handed Poppy a folded note, sealed in red wax. Poppy peered at it. She didn't recognize the seal, or the handwriting.

"Shall I go, miss?"

"Wait for a moment. Let me see what it says, in case I need to send a reply."

Poppy opened the letter, wondering who felt it necessary to disturb her sleep.

Dear Miss St. George,

It may interest you and others close to you to know that Viscount Norbury will engage in a duel related to rumors regarding a blind woman. The men will fight this coming dawn at Darthmore Abbey. I am confident of Norbury's chances, but a prayer or two may not come amiss.

A friend

Poppy laid the letter in her lap, trying to remain calm. The "friend" was obviously Carlos de la Guerra.

While she appreciated the news, she did not appreciate the advice. A prayer! Poppy was growing very sick of waiting patiently as things happened all around them.

"Alice," she said firmly. "One half hour before sunrise, you will wake me and Rosalind, help us dress, and tell John to have the carriage ready in the street."

She didn't explain why, but the maid didn't have to be told. There was only one type of event that was regularly scheduled for dawn. And if Norbury was fighting a duel, the question was, *who was he fighting*?

Alice shivered. "Oh, you can't possibly mean to—"

"Oh, I absolutely mean to. It's the least we can do for Rose, to get to the bottom of this matter. And with any luck, we'll be back before Mr. and Mrs. Blake even wake up. No arguments, now, Alice. Scoot downstairs and keep your mouth buttoned up. We must be very careful until this matter is done."

Poppy sent a very unhappy maid back downstairs, and settled back in her bed. She knew her idea was madcap. But she also knew that if Rose missed this singular chance to understand what was afoot, she'd regret it. And Poppy had no intention of ever letting Rose down.

* * * *

A few hours later, Rose was sleeping like the dead, but was pulled back to consciousness by Poppy, who grabbed her by the shoulder and shook her.

"Get up, Rose!"

"What? What time is it? Is there a fire?" Rose sniffed but smelled nothing other than the candle Poppy must have lit.

"There's no fire in the house, but we may have to put some sort of blaze out. Come, get up! Alice is here to help you dress. We've got to move quickly."

"What is happening?" Rose asked crossly, even as Alice helped her out of bed and began to prepare her outfit.

"I got a message after you went to sleep. Mr. de la Guerra informed us that Norbury is going to fight a duel at dawn."

"A duel! Against who?"

"No idea. That's why I want to go and discover who challenged him and what they know."

"Whoever it is must be desperate," Rose said, briefly muffled as Alice pulled a dress over her head. "Norbury is known to be excellent at dueling."

"Well, someone must think they're better at it. Or they've got a death wish."

"Adrian only fights to first blood," Rose said defensively.

"What if the other man insisted on pistols? First blood could mean death if it hits the wrong place on the body. Are your shoes on yet? Hurry!"

Rose did her best, and soon the girls were creeping through the silent house to reach the front door, where John had called for a carriage, which was now waiting in the street.

He sounded quite upset. "Mr. Blake will have my head if he finds out."

"He won't," Poppy assured him. "We'll tell him that we called for the carriage ourselves. You and Alice go back inside. We hope to be back in an hour, well before anyone else wakes up."

Inside the carriage, Rose could barely sit on the bench

seat. She was now awake enough to fret, and she could only wonder what horrors lay in store at Darthmore Abbey. Was it possible that Adrian could die today? She was furious at him, of course, but she did not want him to die! Nor did she want him to kill.

Oh, men were so difficult! All the nonsense about their honor and who had the right to challenge another, and why did they decide fighting was the answer to everything?

"It must be a man of his class," Rose mused aloud. Adrian would ignore a challenge from a commoner.

"Gentry, at least," Poppy agreed. "But who else would have an interest in rumors about you? This is something only society cares about."

"You're quite certain it is about me? He could be fighting about some other affair."

"No, de la Guerra specially noted it was about you. I don't think he would have bothered to send the message otherwise. After all, it's not as if you could care what happens to Norbury now, correct? You hate him."

There was something sly in Poppy's tone, but Rose disregarded it, because she knew as well as Poppy that whatever she felt for Adrian, it wasn't hate. Fury, rage, hurt, confusion...but not hate.

Aloud, she said, "I just don't want anyone to get hurt on my account."

"*You've* been hurt on your account," Poppy said. "I wish I could fight duels, and then I'd defend your honor myself."

"Poppy, please don't say that. It's bad enough that men act so foolish. Don't you start."

Poppy gave a snort. "I wouldn't be starting, I'd be finishing. Honestly, if women were allowed to defend themselves instead of relying on the nearest male figure who deigns to care, the world would be considerably more peaceful."

"Or all the men would run away in fear," Rose suggested, imagining Poppy with a sword, and finding it all too easy.

"Another way to say more peaceful!" There was a laugh in Poppy's voice, and Rose giggled too.

"Oh, I shouldn't laugh. This is too serious."

"Perhaps it won't be so bad. I know the seconds are supposed to talk just beforehand, and get the parties to come to a resolution before the duel. Something about the prospect of steel in the belly might make the fighters consider their options."

Rose bit her lip. She doubted Adrian would be swayed by last-minute negotiations. She thought of him dying on the green field as the sun broke over the horizon, and shivered.

Poppy leaned over and put her arm around Rose. "Don't worry, I'm sure it will work out, somehow."

"It's the *somehow* that worries me," Rose said. "How far is it?"

"Not far."

"Is it dawn yet?"

"Not yet. But soon. Very soon."

Chapter 24

THE PREDAWN AIR WAS CHILLY, and the mist still clung to the ground, making the scene behind the abbey ghostly and foreboding. Adrian barely noticed, but Carlos carefully stepped on the slick grass, assessing it.

"Wet as if it rained all night," he noted. "I hope you'll keep that in mind."

"Don't fret about the dew. I've fought dawn battles before."

"This morning, though, is a bit different from those previous engagements, is it not?" Carlos looked at him keenly.

"Why?"

"Because this isn't some duel over an affair you conducted under the nose of a dotty noble. This time, you're the one fighting to preserve a lady's honor. Am I right?"

"I fail to see how that will affect my swordsmanship."

"Don't play dumb. You love this girl. Don't let your emotions control you now. Hynes can guess at the truth as well as I can. He'll do what he can to make you lose your wits."

"Have I ever lost my wits?" Adrian asked his friend.

"There's a first time for everything," Carlos noted dryly.

The pair arrived at the avenue of stately elm trees where duels were customarily held just as another carriage pulled up. The man who got out bore a large leather case, marking him as the doctor. He paid the carriage driver, and then hurried toward Norbury and de la Guerra. "Gentlemen," he said. "You appear to be friends, and I don't see anyone else. Is it too much to hope that your opponent has opted out?"

De la Guerra heard the clatter of yet another approaching vehicle at the end of the lane. "Sorry, sir. It appears the coward isn't cowardly enough to not show up."

"I'd hunt him down if he tried to run," Adrian added grimly.

The surgeon looked at him more carefully. "I take it that you initiated this event, my lord. Do you intend to kill your opponent?"

"Fear not, Doctor. I just want to satisfy the demands of honor. Hynes can live, as long as he loses."

The surgeon's lips twisted. "I see." He plainly didn't approve of the whole proceeding.

By that time, Hynes emerged from his carriage and advanced down the lane, dressed in the same clothes as last night. In fact, he didn't look like he'd slept a wink. The only thing to suggest that he'd done any planning was that he had picked up a sword somewhere along the way.

His second walked beside him, now stone-cold sober. He approached Adrian and Carlos immediately, saying, "Mr. de la Guerra. Lord Norbury. I'm not sure we've ever actually been introduced. I'm Derek, Lord Eberling. I don't suppose there's any way to stop this duel from occurring, is there?"

Adrian nodded. "There certainly is. I'll accept an abject public apology from Hynes, addressed to Miss Blake and her parents. He'd also have to agree to give up membership in all his current clubs, which he'd have to do anyway, since he'd get booted from them once they learn of his dealings."

"Go hang, Norbury," Hynes growled as soon as he heard the demands from where he was standing. "I told some stories, that's all. Whoever would have thought that you would turn into a prude?"

"If the stories were only about me, we wouldn't be here. Your mistake was dragging Miss Blake's name into the mud."

"Poor innocent Miss Blake! She can't be that innocent, if she knows you. How's the blind chit in bed, Norbury?"

"For the love of God, Hynes!" said Eberling, disgusted by the insult. He stepped away from Hynes, perhaps reconsidering his whole association with him.

"Is she pregnant with your bastard yet?" Hynes persisted.

Carlos prevented Adrian from attacking Hynes only by throwing himself in between the two men. "Stop it, both of you! You've already agreed to fight a civilized duel!"

He then glared at Adrian. "Calm down," he warned in a low voice. "I told you he was going to try to get under your skin."

"I'm perfectly calm," Adrian growled.

"Walk toward that big elm tree and breathe, you idiot," Carlos ordered. "I'm your second. Let me handle this."

Eberling sighed. "Well, I guess we're not going to get out of this duel after *that* remark. Let's set the rules."

Carlos nodded. "One sword for each man. No other weapons allowed. The duel will continue until first blood is drawn."

"To the death," Hynes declared.

From his position several paces away, Adrian shook his head. "No. I'm not a killer."

"Coward!"

Eberling walked over and grabbed Hynes's arm, whispering something to him. Hynes went a little pale and blinked slowly. After a short conversation, Eberling returned, addressing himself to Carlos, trying to maintain the formality of seconds speaking to seconds.

He said, "We agree that the man who draws first blood is the winner. The loser will immediately drop his sword, and the fight will end. Acceptable?"

Carlos looked at the small circle of men, from the surgeon's somber face, to Hynes and Adrian, both furious, and finally back to Eberling.

"No objections. Let's get this over with, shall we?"

Adrian and Hynes took their places opposite each other in the clearing. At a word from Carlos, both men drew swords. At Eberling's command, they dropped to the *en garde* position, and the duel began.

Adrian had the advantage. He was the better swordsman, he had rest, and he was on the side of *right*, damn it.

Hynes, by his expression, knew it too. He hovered just out of range of Adrian's sword, obviously hoping to tire his opponent and then trick him into making a mistake. Adrian had no intention of letting the fight go that long.

He darted forward suddenly, but slashed only air as Hynes lunged out the way.

"Not as impressive as I'd been told," Hynes sneered. "But you're a lover, not a fighter."

"You'd best focus on my reputation as a fighter," Adrian warned him angrily. He attacked again, but Hynes scurried back quickly, ending up several paces away.

The man in black smiled, showing shark teeth. "We'll

see. If you love like you fight, no wonder you need to resort to romancing cripples." He ducked another swipe of Adrian's blade.

This time, Adrian knew Hynes was deliberately goading him, but he couldn't stop his rage from boiling up. He hated the idea of Hynes even thinking Rosalind's name.

He paused, catching his breath. The tip of his sword dipped momentarily, and Hynes saw it happen. He lunged to press his advantage but found himself fighting a wall of steel. Adrian grinned as he knocked Hynes's sword aside and sliced at his face. A lock of hair fell to the ground. Hynes stared at it in shock.

"*En garde*, Hynes. I don't see a drop of blood. Yet."

Hynes snarled and straightened up. "The only blood you'll see is yours, Norbury."

"I doubt that," Adrian countered. The exchange had restored his confidence. Hynes couldn't beat him fairly, so he had only insults to attack him with. Adrian grew calmer. He had only to wait for the right moment, and then he'd skewer Hynes like a cut of mutton.

Adrian was just deciding where to impale Hynes when all the men heard the distant sound of hoofbeats and the crunch of wheels on gravel. Another carriage was driving through the slowly lifting mist.

"Carlos!" Adrian snapped. "Go tell them to duel somewhere else! This patch is taken."

Carlos and Eberling both started walking to intercept the newcomers. Adrian, who was facing away from the road, kept Hynes firmly in his sights, so he saw when Hynes's eyes widened. He thought it was a trick, but then he heard a voice he'd know anywhere.

It was Rosalind. She was arguing with Carlos, or, more accurately, she was refusing to argue with him. "I am not leaving this field until I speak to Lord Norbury, sir," she was saying.

"He's just a bit busy at the moment, miss," Carlos answered, trying to prevent the two ladies from advancing farther.

"I will wait. I have quite a few things to say to him."

Adrian's heart beat faster. Rosalind should not be here, for so many reasons. How did she even know this duel was happening? Yet she *was* here. She cared enough to come.

He saw no point in wasting more time. He glared at Hynes, and unleashed an aggressive series of thrusts and parries that the other man had no hope to defend against. Within seconds, Hynes was losing ground, gripping his blade with both hands and howling in fury. Adrian was just about to make a tidy slice in Hynes's right cheek when the other man slipped on the dewy ground and lost his balance, stumbling forward as he struggled to avoid falling.

Unfortunately, forward meant running into Adrian's sword, which pierced Hynes's side. Adrian pulled his blade back instantly, but saw that first blood had most definitely been drawn.

The surgeon swooped in just as Hynes slid to the ground, his eyes wide. He gripped his wound until the surgeon could swat his hands away to examine the injury.

Everyone watched, unspeaking, until the surgeon looked up. "A flesh wound. Ugly, but not mortal. The ribs deflected the worst of the strike. With any luck at all, he'll recover swiftly." He then turned back to his patient, intent on his mission.

With that assurance, the other men could focus on the novelty of female observers. Eberling, the only man with no connection to the women, was the first to recover enough to comment. "Who are you? What are you doing here?" he asked, confused. "Ladies must never see this sort of thing!"

"There is absolutely no danger of that, sir," Rosalind replied evenly, facing him with her sightless eyes.

"She's right, for she can see nothing," Poppy noted. "And as far as I can tell, there is no duel going on, just a man who had an unfortunate accident with something pointy."

"I concur," Carlos said. "The young lady has described the scene perfectly. Marvelous luck there was a surgeon handy."

Handing his sword to Carlos, Adrian stepped up to Rosalind, taking her hands in his own. "What brings you out so early, Miss Blake?" he asked, keeping his voice even despite the feelings erupting inside. It was all he could do to not sweep her into his arms right there.

Rosalind shook her head at the light tone, but the strength with which he gripped her hands betrayed his emotion. "I heard you were fighting someone," she replied simply. "Was I supposed to wait patiently to find out if you bled to death?"

"That was precisely what you were supposed to do, though I am glad you ignored convention." He raised one of her hands to his lips, and smiled as he felt her reaction. Then he recalled the matter at hand. "But that still doesn't explain *how* you knew to come." Throwing propriety to the winds, he embraced her. Rosalind was here. What else mattered?

"I received an unsigned letter, telling us about the duel," Poppy explained. "Though it was obvious who sent it. Mr. de la Guerra advocated for us to pray for you, but *I* thought a more direct intervention would be better. Though we barely arrived in time to see the end, and it seems we could not have prevented the fight even if we tried."

"Nevertheless," Carlos said. "It's good to see you."

Poppy frowned at him, but before she could reply, yet another vehicle thundered up the lane, pulling to a stop just behind the hired cab that Poppy had procured.

"Oh, dear," she said in a resigned tone. "It's Mr. Blake. We're all in trouble now."

Chapter 25

❀🌿❀

THE PREDAWN AIR WAS CHILLY, and the mist still clung to the ground, making the scene behind the abbey ghostly and foreboding. Adrian barely noticed, but Carlos carefully stepped on the slick grass, assessing it.

"Wet as if it rained all night," he noted. "I hope you'll keep that in mind."

"Don't fret about the dew. I've fought dawn battles before."

"This morning, though, is a bit different from those previous engagements, is it not?" Carlos looked at him keenly.

"Why?"

"Because this isn't some duel over an affair you conducted under the nose of a dotty noble. This time, you're the one fighting to preserve a lady's honor. Am I right?"

"I fail to see how that will affect my swordsmanship."

"Don't play dumb. You love this girl. Don't let your emotions control you now. Hynes can guess at the truth as well as I can. He'll do what he can to make you lose your wits."

"Have I ever lost my wits?" Adrian asked his friend.

"There's a first time for everything," Carlos noted dryly.

The pair arrived at the avenue of stately elm trees where duels were customarily held just as another carriage pulled up. The man who got out bore a large leather case, marking him as the doctor. He paid the carriage driver, and then hurried toward Norbury and de la Guerra. "Gentlemen," he said. "You appear to be friends, and I don't see anyone else. Is it too much to hope that your opponent has opted out?"

De la Guerra heard the clatter of yet another approaching vehicle at the end of the lane. "Sorry, sir. It appears the coward isn't cowardly enough to not show up."

"I'd hunt him down if he tried to run," Adrian added grimly.

The surgeon looked at him more carefully. "I take it that you initiated this event, my lord. Do you intend to kill your opponent?"

"Fear not, Doctor. I just want to satisfy the demands of honor. Hynes can live, as long as he loses."

The surgeon's lips twisted. "I see." He plainly didn't approve of the whole proceeding.

By that time, Hynes emerged from his carriage and advanced down the lane, dressed in the same clothes as last night. In fact, he didn't look like he'd slept a wink. The only thing to suggest that he'd done any planning was that he had picked up a sword somewhere along the way.

His second walked beside him, now stone-cold sober. He approached Adrian and Carlos immediately, saying, "Mr. de la Guerra. Lord Norbury. I'm not sure we've ever actually been introduced. I'm Derek, Lord Eberling. I don't suppose there's any way to stop this duel from occurring, is there?"

Adrian nodded. "There certainly is. I'll accept an abject public apology from Hynes, addressed to Miss Blake and her parents. He'd also have to agree to give up membership in all his current clubs, which he'd have to do anyway, since he'd get booted from them once they learn of his dealings."

"Go hang, Norbury," Hynes growled as soon as he heard the demands from where he was standing. "I told some stories, that's all. Whoever would have thought that you would turn into a prude?"

"If the stories were only about me, we wouldn't be here. Your mistake was dragging Miss Blake's name into the mud."

"Poor innocent Miss Blake! She can't be that innocent, if she knows you. How's the blind chit in bed, Norbury?"

"For the love of God, Hynes!" said Eberling, disgusted by the insult. He stepped away from Hynes, perhaps reconsidering his whole association with him.

"Is she pregnant with your bastard yet?" Hynes persisted.

Carlos prevented Adrian from attacking Hynes only by throwing himself in between the two men. "Stop it, both of you! You've already agreed to fight a civilized duel!"

He then glared at Adrian. "Calm down," he warned in a low voice. "I told you he was going to try to get under your skin."

"I'm perfectly calm," Adrian growled.

"Walk toward that big elm tree and breathe, you idiot," Carlos ordered. "I'm your second. Let me handle this."

Eberling sighed. "Well, I guess we're not going to get out of this duel after *that* remark. Let's set the rules."

Carlos nodded. "One sword for each man. No other weapons allowed. The duel will continue until first blood is drawn."